I Have Demons

Dear Kathleen and Klaus,
Happy reading during the
long winter months! Thank
you for attending my book
launch!

24 November 2018

I Have Demons

Christopher Adam

IGUANA

Copyright © 2018 Christopher Adam
Published by Iguana Books
720 Bathurst Street, Suite 303
Toronto, ON M5S 2R4

Editor: Holly Warren
Front cover image: Photo by Daniel McCullough on Unsplash
Front cover design: Daniella Postavsky

Issued in print and electronic editions.
ISBN 978-1-77180-300-7 (paperback)
ISBN 978-1-77180-301-4 (epub)
ISBN 978-1-77180-302-1 (mobi)

This is an original print edition of *I Have Demons*.

Contents

Preface   i

An Alpine Lodge Special   1

I Have Demons   36

David and Franco   80

To my family — here and departed

Preface

I Have Demons shines the spotlight on people who, in different ways, live on the margins — the overlooked elderly woman who gets her thrill pocketing stir sticks and coffee creamer; the jaded parish priest tending to the needs of a man holding a terrible secret; and the small-town Ontario student struggling with the very real possibility that his undergraduate degree in literature is a ticket to poverty.

I set out to explore the concept of the centre versus the periphery, alienation, lives lived in futile anticipation, and the brittleness of faith. Writing and reading fiction is such a dynamic process; it is an unspoken conversation between the author and the reader.

Three works have had a particularly lasting impact on me. Margaret Laurence's *The Diviners* is one of the few books I have read and reread many times, even committing to memory one of its incredible monologues — from the scene where the young Morag Gunn accompanies Christie to the Nuisance Grounds where he works. The two were the subject of ridicule for their poverty and unenviable social standing in the fictional town of Manawaka. Yet in a profanity-laced tirade, Christie explains that as the small Prairie town's garbageman, he is privy to the dirty secrets of respectable society — the things that "proper" people most wish to hide about themselves cannot be concealed from him. He is powerful, yet few realize it.

"By their garbage shall ye know them," Christie declares definitively.[1] In a sense, this gruff man of modest means and little formal education was nothing less than a diviner.

Equally meaningful to me was Graham Greene's *The Heart of the Matter*. It's a long journey from a small Prairie town to a British-controlled, colonial West African state. Yet Scobie, a British officer with a conscience so deep that it seems to paralyze him, also appears to be sifting and digging — in his case, he is examining the shallowness of the English colonial community in which he lives and his own troubled Roman Catholic faith, not to mention a debilitating sense of Catholic guilt. This all-encompassing sense of shame and a lack of faith in the power of forgiveness even turns his participation at Sunday Mass into a macabre experience of human loneliness and despair:

> The words of the Mass were like an indictment. [...] there was no joy anywhere. He looked up from between his hands and the plaster images of the Virgin and the saints seemed to be holding out hands to everyone, on either side, beyond him. He was the unknown guest at a party who is introduced to no one.[2]

While Greene explored the concept of guilt and forgiveness within the context of the Catholic faith, twentieth-century Hungarian poet János Pilinszky tackled the presence, or lack thereof, of the Divine in our world against the tumultuous backdrop of postwar Central Europe. Pilinszky produced one of the most powerful works exploring human alienation. The poem "Apocrypha" was borne from the smouldering ruins of the Second World War, the poet's personal experiences in 1945 and a complicated faith in a God who appeared distant and removed from the world of suffering.

---

[1] *Margaret Laurence,* The Diviners, *(Toronto: Bantam Books, 1975), p. 39.*

[2] *Graham Greene,* The Heart of the Matter, *(London: Penguin Books, 1971), p. 223.*

My own word is more homeless than the word.
I have no words. Their terrifying weights
fall crumbling through the air,
a tower rings out and reverberates.

You are nowhere.
The world is but thin air.
Forgotten sun-beds, empty garden chair.
My shadow jars upon the ragged stone.
I stick out of the earth. Worn out. Alone.[3]

Pilinszky, initially barred from publishing during the period of Stalinism in Hungary, spent a lifetime working through the memory and burden of the war, and the Holocaust in particular, but ultimately concluded that

God, exiled from behind the facts, from time to time returns to bleed through the fabric of history. The mark that He leaves is so endlessly unpretentious that it is questionable whether we can ever reach it.[4]

Fractured, often unsatisfying human relationships run through the three stories in this collection. And the human relationship with the Divine is tenuous too. In different ways and taking divergent paths, the characters in each of the stories are in search of redemption.

Ottawa is often synonymous with the federal government, policy wonks, political spin doctors, foreign diplomats, as well as the negative stereotypes of dull stability and mediocrity that haunt government towns. For many, Ottawa is mostly Parliament Hill and the tight political world north of Highway 417. The stories in this collection, however, explore the city's peripheries — both geographic and social. The people in these narratives are not affluent

---

[3] Peter Zollman's translation of "Apokrif" published in the European Cultural Review (no. 14) – The Audit is Done: An Anthology of 20th Century Hungarian Poetry.

[4] János Pilinskzy, *Nagyvárosi ikonok — Összegyűjtött versek 1940–1970* (Budapest: Szépirodalmi Kiadó, 1971), 167. (Excerpt translated by C. Adam)

and, on the surface, they wield little power. Often, they are forgotten and isolated.

Ottawa's landscape lends itself particularly well to exploring the world of the peripheries and of isolation. Beyond the small downtown core of Centretown and the ByWard Market, a handful of adjacent historic neighbourhoods and sprawling suburbia, Ottawa is a vast, sparsely populated land of forests and quiet rural communities on the border between English and French Canada. In these stories, the greenbelt, wilderness and rural life serve various purposes. They are at once places of refuge, sources of redemption, reminders of childhood and innocence, as well as symbols of loneliness and alienation. The people who inhabit or journey to and from these lands in my stories seek both to escape — and at times return — and find comfort.

Christopher Adam

An Alpine Lodge Special

Suzette was in for a treat. She took a quick glimpse at her surroundings before slipping a dozen packets of sugar and a handful of plastic stir sticks into her purse. It was the same ritual every night, except on Sundays. That satisfying little shiver still ran through her body, as if she was pulling the heist for the first time. The old man, even more of a regular at the coffee shop than Suzette, occupied the one family table across from the counter. He squinted at her disapprovingly and made a clicking sound with his tongue. He almost never spoke but still managed to communicate his feelings in no uncertain terms. In all those years, Suzette could remember the old man breaking his silence only once. A few weeks back, the head office installed a self-serve electronic kiosk at each location, after which the franchise owners fired most of the cashiers. That day, the old man rose from his VIP table and demanded to meet with Joel, the young manager, in the dry storage room. Behind closed doors, words flowed endlessly from the old man, one into the other. They were tinged with rage. Suzette could make out only a few — *cold, unwelcoming, impersonal, inhumane.*

"It's way better when he doesn't talk." Joel sounded flustered and Suzette tried to reassure him. The next day Joel and the visibly irritated owner of the franchise location hung a sixteen-by-twenty print of a fireplace in a cozy living room on the wall above the old man.

"Evening, Mrs. Thibeault! You're leaving us already?" Joel towered behind Suzette, who stood facing the soda fountain. She was startled, yet savvy enough to know that she had to remain cool, collected and composed. Those were the three Cs that her son always repeated to her. She calmly zipped up her purse and turned around slowly to the cheerful, pudgy-faced manager. He could have been her grandson. *They are so young these days.*

"Oh, yes, dear. I have a very special dinner tonight." She found that she inadvertently whispered the *very special dinner* part, as if she were preparing to engage in something illicit.

"Nice, nice…" the manager didn't sound too interested, but he also made no move or gesture indicating that he wanted to cut short the conversation. They were in that awkward space where there was nothing more to say, yet neither party seemed willing to assume responsibility for ending the exchange. Maybe he was waiting for her to take the first step. After all, she was much older *and* a lady. Suzette never accepted the accusation that kids these days have no manners. It's true that some of them were never taught proper etiquette at home. And so many young men seemed clumsy and socially awkward. But they were well-intentioned and *very* trainable.

"Before I forget, Joel, the Boston cream was just *wonderful* today. It was so fresh." Suzette smiled, as she buttoned up her coat, leaning into Joel again, lowering her voice, as she said *so fresh*. She never knew why she did that.

"For sure. Guess this time they weren't all freezer burnt when we took 'em out to thaw," remarked Joel with a satisfied smile, pulling his phone from his pocket for no apparent reason. It wasn't ringing. Nobody was texting him. There was no buzz to indicate that yet another virtual friend had "liked" the photo of what he'd eaten for lunch that day. Suzette noticed that young people liked to hold their phones in their hands nowadays. It seemed to give them a sense of security, like an infant clasping a soft, warm blanket.

"Well, I will let you get back to work, *mon minou*. I hope you don't have to stay too late tonight." Suzette turned towards the door. She wanted to get far away from the counter with the soda fountains and the coffee paraphernalia. It was an enclosed space, and the walls, like the old man, had eyes — they had witnessed her act. Her purse felt heavier by the second, as if God was using the burden of her sin to weigh her down.

"Yeah, for sure. See ya tomorrow, ma'am," responded Joel. And within a moment he was buried in his phone.

It was much too cold for early October. The orange hanging lights of the Alpine Lodge, illuminating each booth and window, made the single-storey box building stand out promisingly in the far end of the parking lot. The pavement was uneven, marked with fissures and potholes. Every other moment, a gust of wind felt strong enough to lift Suzette right off the ground and either carry her up through the black starless sky into heaven or toss her right onto the vast four-lane road, where the traffic was relentless.

Everyone was in a rush to get home. A mother frantically packed bags of groceries into her trunk as her infant wailed in his stroller. Her empty shopping cart, taking on a life of its own, made its way down the sloping parking lot, heading perilously towards another parked car. The mother looked up, startled by the sound of the impact. She grabbed her crying infant, now hysterical, plopped him onto the backseat and jumped into the vehicle as quickly as she could, leaving the stroller behind.

"*Madame!*" Suzette raised her voice and looked at the woman in the car, pointing to the abandoned stroller a few feet away. But her words were devoured by the wind and the long growl of a truck ripping down the road. The woman caught a glimpse of Suzette — a slight, almost ghostly presence puncturing an otherwise empty parking lot. She drove away with determination.

**

The Alpine Lodge's washroom was a place of refuge. Suzette felt chilled to the bone, but in this overheated, brightly lit space, with faint remnants of a stranger's perfume in the air, she felt pleasantly ensconced. She reapplied her hallmark red lipstick and emboldened her already rich application of eyeshadow.

"Age gracefully," her son's girlfriend said when they last came down to visit her at the home, a few weeks following her eighty-fifth birthday. Pam's passive- aggressive dig at Suzette's propensity for makeup fell short of a direct order. Pam wasn't invested enough to bark out an order.

Suzette lined her lower eyelid, putting all her mental and physical energy into steadying her hand. The reflection in the mirror made her hands appear particularly gnarly — thin, bony fingers, like bare twigs on a mature shrub after the first frost. Her fingers were attached to what looked like an uneven field with ridges, hills and crevices painted green, blue, purple.

Purple. That's royalty. And royalty, if anything, is graceful. But Suzette was no Queen Elizabeth and she knew it — perhaps more like an ageing actress who once commanded adoring crowds of men and who could still be a captivating presence if she were to return to the limelight. Captivating, yes; though would her audience find her attractive? Suzette gave it a moment of thought before concluding, why *yes*, even if not in the traditional sense.

Suzette stepped away from the mirror, her back up against the stalls. She was getting even thinner and her face seemed to be receding inwards, leaving more pronounced cheeks. Her eyes appeared to have retreated to the backs of their sockets, as if they had just lost a battle. Her ruby lips and her highlighted eyelids shone like car lights piercing through a dark highway. The glitter she had mixed in with her shampoo looked like tiny diamonds shimmering in her hair. The white stockings and short skirt — though unconventional — accentuated what used to be her best feature: her legs.

"Oh my *God*, I think it's really happening this time!" A woman's giddy enthusiasm startled Suzette. She peeked out the washroom door and could see a waitress with a tray of pop in her hands walking away from the line cook, who had stuck his head out of the kitchen. The woman's zeal failed to wash the blank expression off the teenager's pale, almost translucent face.

"Okay, whatever," he replied and ducked back into the kitchen.

"I'm telling you, *this is it*. You just watch me. I'm getting a one-way ticket out of this joint," she added. She hurried towards the tables with a bounce in her step.

Suzette's curiosity was piqued. She certainly didn't want to miss out on anything. For a brief moment, she steadied herself by holding onto the counter before finding the fastest route back to her booth.

***

"Welcome to the Alpine Lodge. My name is Kay. Have you been here before, hon?" The waitress must have been in her early fifties. She had curly red hair, thinning near the top, and wore a black polo shirt bearing a bright Swiss cross and the slogan: *Taking you to new heights.*

"Well hello, Kay. I'm Suzette. And no, I don't believe I have," she replied, eyes sparkling with anticipation.

"Not a problem. Can I start ya off with a drink?" inquired Kay.

"You know, I am right across the parking lot almost every day. They know me there by name. They have wonderful coffee and donuts, but I go for the people and the ambience." Suzette started to laugh, a little self-consciously, as she leaned over to Kay and whispered, "They say I am like a *fixture!*"

"Aw, isn't that nice. Now how 'bout a drink, hon?" Kay stood eagerly with the tip of her pen already sitting on the pages of her notepad, like a marathon runner waiting impatiently on the start line.

"Oh, something nice and warm while I wait would be wonderful, because—"

"Tea? Coffee?"

"You know what, that's a good idea. Maybe a tea!" Suzette sat back in her booth and looked up at Kay, a firm, self-confident and robust presence.

"And I'm guessing you're coming for the traditional turkey dinner special. Am I right?"

"Well yes, Kay. How did you know?" inquired Suzette, genuinely surprised.

"It's what's drawing in new people tonight. The stuffing is to die for. Back in a sec, hon."

Suzette closed her eyes and relished the comfort of the moment. The soft burgundy leatherette bench, the coziness of her very own booth, wooden beams running the length of the ceiling, giving the feeling of a mountain cottage, and a gas fireplace in the middle of the restaurant. *Why didn't I come here sooner?* She saw this place every day from her spot at the coffee shop, and the home was a stone's throw away. She would have just enough left from her pension to treat herself twice a month to a meal fit for a queen, or a respected veteran of Broadway. Either option was more than acceptable to her.

But tonight was different. She was doing this mainly for Mathieu. He could really use a warm meal in a nice family restaurant — probably more than anyone else she knew. A few days ago, yet another dispute with his girlfriend had turned vitriolic. When Suzette called him, poor Mathieu was busy collecting his underwear from atop lampposts and stop signs in Kapuskasing. Pam had driven around town in an awful fury the night before, after their latest fight, using his briefs like Christmas ornaments.

"This is a scandal. Our family has never behaved this way!" No sooner had those words of righteous indignation escaped Suzette's lips, than she realized that perhaps she was being economical with the truth.

"I know, eh?" said Mathieu, sounding as though his thoughts were somewhere else entirely.

"You will drive safely and you will leave early?" asked Suzette. She realized that she had unwittingly wrapped the telephone cord so tightly around her fingers as she was talking that it was cutting off her circulation.

"Yeah," her son responded. *Never a man of many words*, Suzette thought.

"I am taking you to a very special place for a real turkey dinner. Why don't you wear Papa's menthol green turtleneck? It's lovely," she suggested. It was a long-distance call, and her son's response seemed lost in that distance, steadily making its way down nine hundred kilometres of wire to the south.

"It was the best day of my life, when I retired," said the man in the booth across from Suzette.

"*Oui, c'est ça, la.* Elmer there couldn't take de trucking no more," quipped the moustachioed man across from him, who was diligently scraping molecular remnants of stuffing and cranberry sauce off his plate with his fork.

"You know, my son is on the road all the time and I am always worried about him. Timmins one weekend, Sudbury the next," added Suzette.

"You don't have to tell me about that route! I know it like the palm of my hand." Elmer lifted his palm to Suzette, as if he was telling her to stop. She noticed a piece of turkey on the bottom of his middle finger.

"Oh now I don't mean to pry, but you are from the Kap too?" asked Suzette, excited to find someone from back home.

"Nope, but right next to it. Little hole in the wall called Moonbeam," responded Elmer, glaring at his friend with the moustache, who had just poured the last drop of beer from the pitcher into his glass. "Hey, I thought you said that you just wanted a sip, bud?" Elmer added in annoyance. The man shrugged and finally pushed away his empty plate, having ascertained that there was not a speck of turkey dinner left to retrieve.

"Moonbeam!" Suzette glowed. "Oh, that's such a cute place and very special too. A hundred years ago, it was a tiny sign of hope in the endless northern Ontario wilderness. When you finally escape from the darkness of the pine forests, you are greeted by the moon that reflects perfectly off fields of fresh snow. Railway workers thought their eyes, used to darkness, were playing tricks on them, as specks of light mysteriously danced and fell towards them from the night sky — a little like pulsating Christmas lights."

Suzette was lost for a moment in a world forty-five years ago, when the snow made that crunchy noise under her son's boots. Mathieu ran from the woods into the clearing, determined to catch up to Mr. Moon, relaxing placidly before him in a grand navy-blue wing chair, waiting for nobody else but him to finally hop into his lap.

"Cheap real estate." Elmer summoned for the waitress.

"Pardon me?" Suzette felt like she had just woken up and caught a conversation mid-sentence.

Kay walked over with a pot of coffee in her hand.

"You have no idea what to do with all that time on your hands, eh?" She filled up Elmer's cup.

"Well one thing I sure as hell knew was that I couldn't do no more trucking. No siree! It's bad for your prostate, all that sitting ... doctor said. Prostates don't like being squished and pressed up like that all the time, I guess." Elmer waited for his friend with the moustache to back him up, before turning to Kay.

"Now don't you go on blabbing about your private parts! We're not that kind of place, I'll have you know!" Kay turned and glanced at Suzette, who felt like she was on the outside of an aquarium, peering in.

"Are ya still waiting for someone, hon?" Kay's left hand was firmly on her hip, as she held up a coffee carafe with the other hand. It was the quintessential crusty waitress-in-a-diner look. Yet somehow tonight she resembled a stodgier-than-most Greek goddess posing in a statue- maker's studio.

"Oh yes, and would you have a telephone that I could use? I am waiting for my son. He was going to meet me here at seven," she explained.

"Well, it's half past now. You just tell him that if he doesn't get his sweet little *derrière* here in a hurry, he'll be dealing with me, okay, hon?"

Suzette didn't realize that climbing out from one of those booths could be tantamount to a gymnastic feat. She pushed her palms into the table, rose carefully and stood there for a brief moment smiling pleasantly at Kay. It wasn't the first time she used a meticulously timed pause and a warm facial expression to draw attention away from her limp.

"Kitchen closes at nine. Just sayin'!" Kay kept her hand firmly on her hip while Suzette made her way to the front.

***

Suzette realized she was doing that thing again with the telephone cord, so she stopped.

"And how have you been, Pam?" Suzette inquired.

"Never better." Pam's voice was flat. Not even enough energy and umph for it to classify as muted sarcasm.

"I am so worried about poor Mathieu, you know. He was supposed to be here at seven. The roads are terrible, just terrible," noted Suzette.

"I wouldn't blame the roads for this one. I mean, has he *ever* been on time?"

"But he knows that this is a very special dinner in a nice restaurant…" Suzette was incredulous that the delay could be down to anything other than the miserable state of Highway 17 when the autumn evening rain began freezing on the pavement.

"Yeah and he also knows where to stop for a good time along the way…" Suzette decided not to dignify that comment with a response. "Or maybe someone knocked a little good sense into him and he decided to sleep off his hangover on the side of the road," Pam added, with incrementally rising bitterness.

"I know my son, Pam," Suzette said quietly.

"Oh, believe you me, I know him too. Listen, Dillon's screaming in the tub. I gotta go. I hope it works out for you tonight. Don't let him feed you any of his bullshit."

And Pam was gone. As usual, no good-bye. Nobody ever taught her it's only polite to say good-bye to people, otherwise your last sentence is just left dangling. Incomplete.

Suzette leaned over the counter. As she put the phone down, she could see Kay finishing a small bowl of pudding in the kitchen while waiting for the boy to complete an order.

"I know you don't give a damn about this. And you probably don't even believe me. But you just watch me. I'm outta here."

"Good." The boy punched some numbers on the microwave.

"Oh, you're gonna miss me. You just wait and see. Fabio's sending me the first installment of my payout tonight at nine. Just the first of many. Once the first bit hits my account — and let me just say that it's more than what you've ever come across in your piddling nineteen years on this earth combined — I'll be storming outta here so fast your pin-shaped head will spin. Hold on tight, sugar bits!" Kay took one big lick of her spoon and tossed it two metres away into the sink. *Hell*, thought Suzette, *she could be a basketball star if she wanted.*

"So why are you so sure of everything?" The boy seemed semi-interested as the microwave gave off its customary ding.

"Do you drink water?" Kay folded her arms.

"Um, *yeah*. Like everyone," the boy said, clearly thinking Kay's question was stupid.

"Good. And so do the poor bastards in South Africa ... except they've run out of water. Some of them are already lining up for hours on street corners with plastic containers to get some from public taps. Water's a bigger commodity over there than gold. You can sell off your gold engagement ring to dirty Ted's pawn shop, but you can't do shit when your taps are bone dry."

The boy was giving her his undivided attention, but it was impossible to tell whether he found the situation in South Africa or the reference to dirty Ted more captivating.

"The government is *literally* telling people to stop flushing their toilets, to take two-minute stop-start showers or stand in a pail to save their bath water and reuse it." The boy looked disgusted as he reached for his cellphone for no apparent reason. "If it's yellow, let it mellow. That might as well be South Africa's national motto these days," Kay added.

"So what's this Fabio guy doing for you?" The boy feigned interest as he searched for a new text message.

Kay walked over to the boy and patted him on the head.

"That's the million-dollar question, kiddo. Fabio's a genius. He perfected desalinization in South Africa, and his timing was spot on." The boy looked at Kay with an expression as blank as a freshly wiped whiteboard.

"He sucks the salt out of the seawater, you douche! Imagine turning the goddamned Atlantic into one big open bar! I helped him out a bit with the start-up costs — you know, because of my trust in him and for a few other favours. Yeah, so now he's giving me a handsome cut of his profits." Kay leaned up close against the boy and whispered, "One third."

"Yeah?" Something piqued and even sustained the boy's interest. "But seawater ... *man* ... doesn't that smell like rotting garbage?"

***

"French Canadian split pea soup. Thought you'd like it." Kay placed the cup of soup and a pack of soda crackers in front of Suzette, who was genuinely stunned. "On the house, hon. Kitchen closes in a little over an hour, so why let it go to waste?"

"Oh, well thank you so much, dear — that's such a lovely gesture!" Suzette stirred the soup with her spoon, looking for the little chunks of ham. She counted at least four and was genuinely impressed. It pays to have a meal at a *real* restaurant once in a while.

"So where's that son of yours?" Kay sounded as though she was holding Suzette accountable, but in fact she had it in for Mathieu. What kind of son stands up his poor old mother like that on Thanksgiving?

"Oh, he leads a very hard life," Suzette said, though she knew she was making excuses for him. "I know he will be here any minute now."

"You give me a weekend with Matty boy, and I'll whip his ass into shape, in either official language!" Kay startled Suzette as she slapped a kitchen cloth against the table, a mere five inches from her soup. "Then again, chances are I'll be ditching this place pretty soon, so you won't find me here. You'd have to hire a mobster to come scrape me off the beach in Varadero and drag me back to O-Town."

Suzette only realized now that she was starving. She meticulously blew a little air on the first spoonful of soup before putting it in her mouth. She would have preferred every mouthful in peace, but she could tell that Kay was waiting for a response. And the soup was free, so she certainly deserved that much from her.

"Yes, you know I must admit that I overheard a little of what you were saying to that young man in the kitchen and, well—"

"I tell you, it's the best decision I have ever made in my life. It cost me a pretty penny, but the returns, *the returns!*" Kay looked over at Elmer and Moustache; both of them seemed subdued after their second pitcher of beer, or maybe they had gotten to a point in their friendship where they had nothing left to say to each other.

"What are you thinking, love?" Kay wiped her dish cloth on Elmer's mostly bald head. A small handful of unruly, excessively long strands of hair stood up at attention.

"Won't be the same without her, eh?" Elmer glanced at Moustache who was masterfully rolling up a dirty napkin into what Kay thought looked like a tight, fresh joint.

"I bet I'm the only woman to touch you like that, am I right?" Kay wiped Elmer's bald scalp again with the rag. He smiled mischievously.

"You wanna drive up with me to Moonbeam? I can take a nice girl like you to the moon and back, you better believe it." Elmer glanced over at Suzette for a reaction, but she was still working diligently on her soup.

"Unless the man in the moon goes by the name of Fabio and has a nice fat cheque for me, I'd say you can stuff it, sweet pea." Kay turned around and marched back to the kitchen. It offered the best vantage point of the restaurant. The little old lady was hunched over that cup of soup. It should have taken only a few minutes to eat. Elmer and Moustache were still sitting in silence, though she could swear that the back of the old man's head looked shinier than before. And in the far end of the restaurant, Mme. Charbonneau was poking the half-eaten *tarte au sucre* on her plate, mostly out of boredom, while her husband went on a digging expedition in his teeth with a toothpick.

Kay found it all a bit sad, really: she had spent the last fifteen years of her life working at a restaurant that attracted mostly French Canadian pensioners from the neighbourhood, truckers passing through and only the occasional tourists from overseas who strayed too far east of Parliament Hill. Had she worked at one of those snooty places in the ByWard Market or Westboro, catering to pompous men who called themselves foodies, maybe she wouldn't be bored to death with her lot in life. She might be inclined to smack them, but her days would be undeniably more colourful.

It was time to go. Just plain time. The Alpine Lodge was slow-acting poison to her. And truth be told, she was probably lethal to the place as well. The time had finally come to make that phone call to Fabio. It was still the early hours of the morning over in Cape Town, but a guy like him was sure to be wired day and night.

***

"Ma'am, there's a Matthew on the phone for you…" The boy from the kitchen stood awkwardly at Suzette's booth, with his right thumb in his belt, shifting his weight from one foot to the other. He avoided most interaction with guests. He was fine in the kitchen and he'd grown accustomed to Kay, but he seemed to freeze up and had trouble swallowing whenever he had to deal with clients. But Kay was on the phone in the storage room and he knew all too well not to disturb her when she was in there.

Suzette's eyes lit up and she even surprised herself by hopping out of the booth with near acrobatic ease. As she approached the receiver of the phone, lying on the plastic countertop, she could hear two tinny voices on the line.

"*Mon pitou*, where are you?" Suzette became aware of what sounded like an argument from behind the locked door of the storage room.

"Mom, look — I'm running into some problems here tonight." Mathieu cleared his throat and there was a voice mumbling something in the background. "I had a flat tire just outside Deep River…"

Suzette felt her heart sink. The hopeful anticipation that had her fired up all day, like a diesel engine, just oozed out of her, gathering in a pool on the linoleum.

"Are you all right? Oh, this is awful — you know, the kitchen in the restaurant is closing soon! What are we going to do now? I suppose we can go next door and have a sandwich or doughnut and I have some fresh fruit in my room. But, Mathieu — Thanksgiving is ruined!"

"No worries, Mom. I'll be there first thing in the morning, I promise. I'll find a motel for the night and I'll leave real early in the morning — like at six. We could go for brunch, eh?"

Of course, Suzette was happy to see her son any time, but she wasn't sure how many Thanksgivings she had left. At eighty-five, you couldn't take anything for granted. She stood with the receiver in her hand, somehow unmotivated to even respond. Her mind felt foggy and it took her a minute to realize that she was staring blankly at the boy in the kitchen. He was sitting on a stool, buried deep in his phone and oblivious to her. He was near the end of his shift, the restaurant was winding down for the night and Suzette hadn't eaten dinner yet.

She wasn't hungry, but that was nothing new. In fact, had Mathieu arrived as expected, chances are she would have sat there pushing her food from one end of the plate to another, watching her son devour whatever was placed in front of him. She wasn't really here for the food, as such. God knows she'd had plenty of turkey, cranberry sauce from a can and mediocre pre-prepared stuffing in her life. She was here to give her son something special, to bring a degree of normalcy to that mess of a life he led, but also to get away from the home. And maybe deep down she was even trying to show Joel from the doughnut shop across the parking lot that she was more than just a fixture and that he shouldn't take her for granted. She had places to be and people to meet.

Her thoughts were cut off abruptly when Kay appeared from the storage room. She leaned against the door, rubbed her temples and began chewing the nail on her thumb.

"Can I help you?" Kay looked at Suzette, not really seeing her.

"Well, it seems like my son's car had a defect on the road and he won't make it tonight. I'm so sorry for the trouble — I know you were expecting two at our table…"

Kay waved her hand, indicating that she wasn't bothered.

"But I would love to try your Thanksgiving special; I have heard such good things about it! Of course, only if it's not too late."

"It's fine. Go on back to your table. I'll have it out in a couple of minutes." Kay turned to the boy, who was still texting.

"I need you to get me one more special and then you can call it a night…" The boy glanced up at Kay and seemed to be examining her.

"What's up?" he responded.

"I just told you *what's up*! Do all you lazy, entitled, good-for-nothing millennials need to be spoon-fed? You want me to text it to you?" Kay looked like a raging lion — her red curly hair framing a rounded face, intense eyes that could cut through human flesh and nostrils expanding and inflamed with anger.

"Holy shit! Get a grip…" The boy got up from the stool and walked over to the counter. "So, what did your friend Fabio say?" Kay kept a distance as the boy used an ice cream scoop to plop a serving of stuffing onto the plate.

"When did I say we were friends? We're business partners…" Kay was annoyed, though slightly deflated.

"Or fuck buddies, eh?" The boy chuckled as he put the finishing touch on the plate: a healthy serving of gravy over the slightly dry turkey and an unruly mound of lumpy mashed potatoes. For a split second, he was satisfied with himself; but it was a fleeting moment — a salt shaker went flying towards him, slamming into the wall a mere foot from his head.

"What the…? Oh yeah, you're *definitely* losing it."

"Is everything okay in there?" Elmer emerged from the washroom. He was walking like a penguin — belly distended, thick bifocal glasses continually sliding down his nose and those desperate strands of hair on an otherwise bald scalp still reaching for the sky.

Kay ignored him and waved Elmer away dismissively. She turned to the boy.

"I couldn't get a hold of Fabio. Some floozy picked up the phone. He hadn't come home in three days and she didn't know where he was. And she didn't have the brains to ask around. He's on some business trip, he told her, but not a word more." Kay poured herself a glass of ice water from the plastic pitcher.

"What about his cellphone?" asked the boy, who began to feel like he was a detective in a mystery.

"It's turned off. And his voicemail is full…" Kay spat out the ice cube that she had been sucking back into the glass. She was feeling increasingly disoriented — just not herself at all.

"Shit, eh? Here, why don't you take this to the old lady over there, and in the meantime, I'll see what I can find…"

Kay was taken aback. Did the boy just order her to do something? She stared at him for a second with piercing eyes and a vexed expression, before grabbing the plate.

***

Suzette was eating her Thanksgiving dinner in silence. Someone had turned off the background music. She didn't really notice it until it was gone. But it had filled the empty spaces in the restaurant, making the pauses in human speech a little more comfortable. All that was left was Elmer absent-mindedly tapping the nail on his pinkie against the plastic pitcher. He wished that it was not devoid of beer, but he was too tired to order another.

As Suzette swallowed, each bite of turkey and stuffing seeming to gather like a smooth, miniature golf ball at the back of her throat, before finally going down into her stomach. It was the same feeling she would get when they surreptitiously rolled one of her neighbours in the home on a stretcher through the back door.

She was not quite ready to cry but too upset to speak or eat. Still, the food was lovely and she felt strangely at home here, even though this was her first time at the Lodge. She could see herself coming back again and again, getting to know the characters a little better each time, until they became like family — with all their idiosyncrasies and imperfections. Suzette reconsidered that for a moment. No. They would not be like family — more like the characters of a never-ending soap opera, the ragtag lot of *Coronation Street*, who grow on you with time, until they begin to occupy an important place in your daily life. You get to know them, you know all of their faults and their messy lives. You are free to observe them, compare your lot in life to theirs, and eventually, you pretend to be a part of their world.

Kay had just handed the Charbonneaus their bill and, as usual, M. Charbonneau furtively slipped her five dollars while his wife hobbled to the washroom. That was always above and beyond the tip. His wife controlled the family credit card, but M. Charbonneau always had some extra cash in his pocket. They never really engaged Kay the way that Elmer and Moustache did. And M. Charbonneau felt more like a kindly grandfather giving his granddaughter a fiver to buy herself a chocolate bar and a medium slush at the convenience store. It made her smile. She was never that proverbial sweet girl with the ponytails and a docile disposition. Not then and not now. If anything, she had been a terror who transitioned into the cantankerous middle-aged grouch that she was now.

M. Charbonneau asked for only one thing in exchange for a five: after each meal, he would take out a handful of small photos of his granddaughter from his wallet. Rosalie was the gem in their family. Kay never actually met the little girl, but through these photos, she followed her along every milestone in her young life — birthday parties, school plays, first communion, apple picking. This time, Rosalie's grandfather had something extra special — a storybook that the ten-year-old girl illustrated and wrote for a school project.

Kay's French was passable at best, but she understood the laminated picture book perfectly. It was a story about a little girl, scared to death of water, who had gotten lost in a forest. She could leave the woods only if she swam across a raging river. The helpless girl lay curled up on a bed of autumn leaves, despairing that she might never escape the woods. As she lay there paralyzed, a caribou sat down next to her on the leaves. Not a word was exchanged between the two of them, yet the girl knew that the caribou was there to help her cross the river. They made their way to the water together, the little girl mounted the animal and the caribou began swimming with determination across the roaring river, transporting the girl to safety. Once on the other side, the girl and the caribou stood in silence, mesmerized by the flickering lights in the distance. The girl was almost home, but the caribou could never inhabit her world. He took one long look at the girl, committing her to his memory, and then without a word made his way back to the water.

"Well now..." Kay seemed lost for words. "That's sweet. Really sweet. You've got yourself a winner here, love." M. Charbonneau smiled in satisfaction. Kay kept holding that book for another moment. She abruptly opened it back up a second time, flipped through the pages and ran her fingers over the smooth texture of the paper. For a moment, the warm waxy scent of coloured crayons blocked out the smell of reheated food. But Kay knew that she had to face the boy in the kitchen.

As Kay walked in, the boy stood there facing her and raised his cellphone screen, shining brightly in the dingy kitchen, close to her face.

"And what exactly do you want me to do with that? I left my glasses at home and I sure as hell can't read that print." She slammed her empty tray on the counter. "Just tell me what it says." Kay stared at a scuffed-up cupboard door, with no desire to look at the boy and his phone. She felt a "told you so" was in the works and the last person she'd tolerate that from was some socially awkward pimply kid.

The boy usually hated reading aloud, but this time he was filled with a mix of nervous anticipation and pride. He had gotten to the bottom of the mystery and it was not *he* who had fallen for some stupid scam, but rather his overly self-confident, always right, wannabe bully of a co-worker. He cleared his throat. His voice broke when he read the first words, but as he kept on reading the story, he felt like a veteran news anchor — the old woman his parents had been watching on CTV every night for as long as he could remember.

"Authorities seize bank accounts and assets of Cape Town confidence trickster Fabio Smuts. Smuts, charged with three counts of wire fraud, identity theft and uttering threats, vanished from Cape Town on Wednesday after withdrawing nearly five million rand from his bank account over the past few days. Smuts is believed to have swindled mostly elderly women from Australia, the United Kingdom and Canada out of millions of rand, with promises of getting rich on Cape Town's water crisis. Smuts claimed to have perfected a groundbreaking new process for turning seawater into drinking water. It was this plan and Smuts' reported charisma and romantic allure that successfully deceived the women. Many are now frantically urging South African authorities to help them recover their lost savings…"

The boy paused. Kay was still facing the cabinets, motionless.

"The story goes on…"

"Enough." Kay crossed her arms.

The boy stared at the back of her head. As he noticed her thinning hair, he reflected, *I thought that only happened to men.*

"This really sucks…" The boy wasn't sure what would be the right thing to say in a situation like this. And knowing Kay, he was worried she would turn around suddenly and attack if he said the wrong thing. "So … like how much are you out?"

"Enough. You saw the story with your own eyes, didn't you?" She continued facing away from the boy. "Sunshine here swindled foolish, sexed-up old women out of all their savings. There you have it. I'm going for a smoke." Kay fumbled in her pocket for a moment and then stormed out of the kitchen and restaurant.

***

Suzette finished only half the food on the plate. *Portions seem to double in size every decade or so*, she thought. But she could not allow for the leftovers to go to waste. She wasn't exactly excited about eating the microwaved remains from a Thanksgiving dinner tomorrow — a dinner that did not go according to plan — but turning up at the home with a big rectangular Styrofoam container said something. It said that she was still vital enough to go out on her own, to decide her own meals, to come and go as she pleased. It would send a message to the nurses and orderlies, as well as to other residents. Well, the residents who were still lucid. Kay had left suddenly, so she couldn't wave her down. And that shy young man in the kitchen didn't look up long enough from his phone to notice Suzette stretching her neck, trying to attract his attention.

"Almost everything's good about the Lodge, except they don't let you leave," mumbled Elmer. Moustache took no notice. His head was on his placemat; he was bored out of his mind, but too lazy or tired to really want to get up and leave.

Suzette smiled at Elmer. "Well, I really enjoyed myself so much tonight. Everything was just lovely. But the night staff at the home are going to start worrying about me…"

Elmer blew his nose in a napkin and turned to Suzette.

"Sorry about your son being a no-show and all. You raise them for eighteen years, support them for another ten and then they dump you like a dirty dish rag, eh?" Elmer shook his head before throwing a sugar packet at Moustache. The man casually gave him the finger but kept his head on the table.

Suzette wanted to explain that Mathieu was actually a wonderful son and how she was looking forward to brunch with him tomorrow morning. But then the young man from the kitchen showed up suddenly from behind.

"Can I wrap that up for you, ma'am?" He didn't seem to know what to do with his hands when he was talking with someone, so he started biting his nails.

"Oh, you read my mind, dear! Please…" She passed him her plate. "And, I don't mean to pry, but is everything fine with sweet Kay? She left so suddenly…"

The boy rubbed his eyes. "Yeah, she's a little upset. But she'll come through."

Suzette's curiosity was at its peak and she was getting her second wind too — she'd arrived at the border of the land of sleep, but her body suddenly decided to make a sharp U-turn.

"She was just as excited as I would be if I believed that I had won the lottery! I hope it all ends well for her…" Suzette smiled at the young man who just shook his head and grimaced awkwardly.

And then like a bomb going off, the door to the restaurant flung open and there stood Kay, a dominating presence that could make the building shake. She looked at the boy with fierce, determined eyes.

"How 'bout you give me some good news tonight! Do we have any stuffing left?"

The boy looked at her nervously. "I think there's like half a pan left in the kitchen … on top of the stove…"

Kay marched into the kitchen with the determination of a sergeant. She re-emerged in less time than it took to take a deep breath, holding a large metal pan of stuffing in her hands. She dropped it onto the counter from two feet up, making an ominous thud. Mme. Charbonneau put her hand over her mouth before grabbing her husband's arm. Elmer's jaw dropped and stayed there, while Moustache raised his left eyebrow. Suzette, startled at first, stretched her neck to get a better view. The restaurant went quiet: the Charbonneaus were standing with their coats on, ready to leave, while Suzette, Elmer and Moustache seemed almost huddled together on the other side. The boy just stood next to Suzette, with his mouth slightly open and a plate of half-eaten turkey dinner in his hands.

"All right, folks — listen up!" Kay stood behind the counter. Her voice had become gritty and rough. She sounded like she had spent the last hour yelling. "It turns out that I'm in the giving mood these days. Hell, it turns out that I'd happily give my right arm to help my fellow man. You can suck my veins dry, take my last penny and I'd just hop, skip and jump on over to the poorhouse. That's me, you know! Caring Kay!" She was roaring and her face turned the colour of her hair; the artery in her neck throbbed and beads of sweat collected at the corners of her forehead, just waiting to escape from captivity in one grand drip and run all the way down to her chin.

Suzette found that she was both concerned and transfixed. She was concerned that this poor, hard-working woman was going to do something she would later deeply regret. But she was also enthralled. It was like she was right in the middle of a television show. She wasn't shielded by a screen and she wasn't just a nameless consumer, light years away. She was in the thick of it. And she might even become an active participant in whatever would unfold.

"Well then, who wants seconds? Or thirds?" All eyes were on Kay and not a person moved or made a sound. "Come one, come all! This is your chance! It's on the house tonight and if the managers of this joint give me hell afterwards, they can just deduct it from my paycheque. So no sweat, folks! Come on up!" Kay sounded as though she were a magician at a county fair inviting little children to come up for free lollipops at the end of a performance.

Kay stood there examining the room with a fierce intensity and smile that exposed all her teeth. Her head, hair and body were visibly worn by the passage of time, but her teeth were lily white — like a necklace made of ivory cubes.

Moustache adjusted himself a little in his chair, cleared his throat and spoke in an uncertain voice as he glanced at Elmer and Suzette. "I guess I'd take some…" He seemed apologetic to the people around him, as if he had broken a blood oath between them not to accept anything and, by doing so, would bring disaster on the whole nation.

"Well that's just grand. *Grand!*" Kay roared. She wiped her face with her hands, revealing a smile that had morphed into a snarl.

Moustache was about to get up from his chair when Kay put her right hand out, signalling for him to stop dead in his tracks. She spoke with a voice that sounded soothing on the surface but concealed a reservoir of hostility that could turn into aggression at a moment's notice.

"Sweet pea, we here at the Alpine Lodge believe in quality service and a first-class dining experience, where the sky's the limit. So how about you just sit the fuck down and let me take care of you, okay?"

Moustache slunk back into his booth. Elmer broke the silence.

"I think maybe you're a little beat, Kay … I mean, it's been a long night and you've been on your feet for hours non-stop…" Elmer paused and looked at the boy standing frozen between his booth and Suzette's. "So how about we call it a night and, uh, you'll see a real generous side of me when I tip." Elmer forced a laugh, but in the nervous silence of the restaurant, it echoed unpleasantly off the walls.

Kay took a deep breath and let out a primal scream that seemed to last an eternity — the sort of scream that the raging person knew very well would solve nothing yet felt immensely satisfying.

"You want some generosity on the side, hon? Well then, Kay is *at your service!*" And with that, Kay dug both hands into the stuffing and filled her mouth to the point where her face appeared ready to burst. She tilted her head back and with her body functioning like an industrial ventilator of monstrous proportions or a canon exploding, the stuffing went catapulting through the air towards the guests.

Elmer, Moustache and the kid ducked. The Charbonneaus pushed their backs against the wall, hoping to disappear into the panels. But Suzette, tinier than anyone else in the restaurant, sat upright in her booth, eyes turned towards the ceiling, mesmerized by bright-green specks of celery, bits of red peppers, translucent chopped onions and chunks of soggy bread cubes that looked like snow jetting above her. It felt almost festive. She didn't turn around to see where the stuffing landed and she couldn't explain how it managed to fly so far.

The boy noticed two things:

1.   The old lady in the booth looked like she had just personally experienced a sublime Christmas miracle.

2.   Three security cameras were pointing right at them. They were sure to capture Kay's performance. When the owners saw this, Kay and he would both be out of a job.

He mustered up some courage and glared at Kay, with eyes wide open, trying to communicate some kind of warning. He nudged his head ever so slightly towards one of the security cameras, and Kay, who was scooping up another load of stuffing with her hands from the pan, noticed him. She slammed the stuffing back into the pan and placed her hands firmly on her hips.

"Oh, now *look at that*. Sugar's about to wet his pants..." Kay glared at the boy, but for a fleeting moment, her better judgment checked in — only to pack up and seek refuge just as quickly. Not too far below the surface, she knew that this was madness. But she also realized that it was too late to turn back. What's done is done. There's no point in stopping halfway to worry about turning back on that one-way road to hell. She couldn't just retrace her steps and pretend none of this ever happened. As far as she was concerned, she might as well put her foot on the gas and tear right down that road like a terror. Besides, it was always entertaining to watch the reactions of prudish women — palms over their bosoms in righteous indignation at the horror of it all. Then again, she could tell that little old Suzette wasn't that kind of woman at all. Seemingly fragile and very thin, yes, but she sure as hell had a mischievous fire burning in that scrawny little body.

Kay erupted in an enraged laugh. The windows of the Alpine Lodge vibrated for a couple of seconds as her sound filled the space and bounced off the walls.

"I know just what you guys need. You need a *real* show, something meaty … something to really sink your teeth into, something *satisfying…*" Kay found herself staring at Elmer, who sat with his mouth slightly ajar and with a seemingly vacant or at least helpless expression. He looked over to Moustache, mostly a silent type.

"*Ta-bar-nac…*" He spoke slowly and softly, each juicy syllable of the word rolling off his tongue in disjointed little pieces. Then he put the toothpick back into his mouth and returned to staring at his placemat.

"As you folks can probably tell, I'm no pussy willow. Hell, anyone who is wouldn't make it through a week of waitressing. I'm going on twenty years. *Twenty years…*" Kay dug her right hand deep into the pan of stuffing next to her.

"How 'bout we end this night with a bang, eh? I think this calls for a little Tammy Wynette and some spicy dancing on my part. Consider it my little parting gift to all of you — including *you*, kiddo." The boy took a step back. He didn't mean to, but it was like his needle-thin body instinctively knew that it was best to retreat. "Yup, this is for you too — I bet at your age, anything would get you off nice and quick."

Kay turned around and hunted in a shoebox full of CDs, behind the counter. All the guests in the restaurant seemed frozen and silent — except perhaps Suzette. She fidgeted and stretched her neck to see what Kay was going to do next. Until now, she thought that nothing could beat the thrill she experienced when pocketing stir sticks and sugar packets — enough to now fill an entire drawer in her room. She was coming to the climax of the finale of a long-running soap, broadcast in 3-D. And she was right in the thick of it. But that internal voice of reason and good judgment that often grows stronger with maturity was making itself heard through all the excitement as well.

Poor Kay is such a hard-working woman, but whatever she was hoping for tonight must have gone so wrong. Suzette looked around at the others in the restaurant. Everyone seemed wrapped in isolated shells of awkward silence. People avoided eye contact with each other. They behaved like an audience that came to a stand-up comedy night but then realized halfway through that the performance was taking an unexpectedly eerie and freakish turn. Kay was fumbling with the CD player at the front as the realization dawned on Suzette that she had to do something. Kay was becoming a pathetic spectacle, and it looked like things were about to get worse.

Kay turned around from the CD player with something between a smile and a snarl, just as the song "Stand by Your Man" started playing. It began slow and slightly whiny — a humdrum, tawdry country tune working its way up to a melodramatic climax in the refrain. As Wynette ruminated about the centuries-old burden of being a woman faced with men who just can't help themselves, Kay mounted the counter and stood up straight for a moment, before she methodically pulled off her nylons. The faces in the audience became blurry — blank ovals attached to sad bodies. She swung her nylons over her head like a lasso and gyrated her hips. *It'll land where it lands*, she thought. She gave it one last twirl and then let it go. But it didn't fly far, landing unceremoniously on the tile a few feet from the boy.

Well that fell flat, Kay thought, disappointed, but she didn't have much time to mourn her failed gesture of sensuality. Wynette's voice was curling through the refrain a second time when a slight figure moved ever so precariously towards the stage. A few steps later, she could see it was the old French lady, walking tentatively, with her arms raised on either side to stabilize her, like a ghost hiding under bed linens.

"*Mon trésor*, let me join you!" Suzette glanced up at Kay, who towered above her on the counter. Kay looked like Lady Liberty, but would she decide to look down for a moment from her frozen forward stare to hear a request from her people? Suzette whispered, as though she sought to partake in something exciting, and which she also knew was illicit.

Kay felt paralyzed. This scrawny old lady had stopped her in her tracks. And now she wants *what*? Kay ran her fingers through her hair and noticed that the texture was thinner again at the top than the last time she had checked it.

"Well, fuck it. Why the hell not."

Suzette pondered for a second on how to mount the stage. Kay pointed to a plastic stool next to the cash register. Suzette hurriedly made her way over, climbed the wobbly stool — *oh, the head nurse at the home would never approve of this; if only she could be here!* — took one big step, lifting her leg up to an angle that she had thought to be surely impossible and suddenly found herself on top of the world. She looked at her public and smiled graciously. They sat there so still. What a disciplined lot, what a *wonderful* audience! Everyone seemed to be holding their breath in anticipation of the next act. Suzette almost forgot about Kay, but she came to her senses as soon as she turned to the waitress standing next to her. She didn't seem quite as tall now, nor nearly as confident. Wayward strands of hair were clinging to her sticky forehead. She looked tired, confused.

"All righty then, I guess it's all yours honey..." Kay waved her hands, seemingly in defeat. This was enough to bring Suzette crashing back to reality and to her mission here.

"No, no! You're not done yet, my dear! You know it's the finale that everyone here will remember most from the performance, from this gift that you gave us this evening. We could have all had our turkey in silence, just filling our stomachs with food to survive and going home from this … this evening chore. No! You gave us more. You shook us up and *woke* us up!" Suzette's pupils were a vivid indigo blue, staring at Kay with impassioned intensity.

Kay put her hands on her hips and stared, bemused, at the little old woman next to her on the counter.

"Are you for real, lady?" She glanced at the blank oval faces, still sitting motionless atop all these ill-proportioned bodies. Something in her wanted one of those ovals to nod at her, discretely indicating that it was okay and that they agreed with the old woman's assessment. Everything would be just fine. But she got nothing. She looked for the boy but couldn't find him. He was missing in action. Typical.

Suddenly, Kay could feel a cold, bony hand gently wrap itself around her elbow.

"*Mesdames et Messieurs*, the final act tonight is a simple but lovely ballroom dance featuring the enchanting Mademoiselle Kay!" A beaming Suzette turned from her public to Kay, who still had an expression of disbelief painted on her face. "Dear, go turn off that CD and set the radio to 98.4 FM. We'll still catch a bit of *The Flying Forties Evening Lounge*. It's music from before your time, but you'll just love it!" Suzette was whispering, as though she was sharing a secret tip that she didn't need the whole world knowing about.

Kay stood frozen, just staring at the energetic old lady. Then she turned to the CD player sitting at the far end of the counter. "Well, it's no skin off my back…"

The smooth, dreamy sounds of the forties seeped into the restaurant, like warm water rolling up to all four corners of a porcelain tub, filling a previously cold space with a coziness that gives you goosebumps. She could hear the deep, sensual voice of a chain-smoking woman singing, but for some reason could not make out most of the words, except for the refrain:

Climb down to me from your star,
Through your fields of satin, carry me afar.
Soothe me with your cool midnight embrace.
Free me from this entangled web of lace,
Let me saunter with you on the soft surface of space…

Lost in the refrain, Kay didn't even notice that the old lady was leading her through the steps of a ballroom dance. Her grandmother was the last person to lead her in the box step — almost four decades ago — on the middle of that ratty old Persian rug in the den, the one sprinkled with breadcrumbs, grape seeds and the odd safety pin. She had so much patience. *Feet together. Watch where you put your weight. Left foot forward. Check your weight again. Now the right. Feet together. Now do all of that backwards.*

Suzette flowed. Kay was choppy. Suzette was barely conscious of her movements; they came naturally. Based on the expression on her face, her beautiful blue Boeing 747 had just landed safely in some distant, dreamy world and she was waltzing homeward bound over the tarmac. Kay was very much still here in this world, but something had changed. At first, she couldn't pinpoint what it was. Was it the plastic counter that felt somehow wider than it should — a veritable, grand dance floor? — No, it wasn't that, though it was a bit surreal and she couldn't quite explain why they hadn't fallen off the narrow strip yet. The room around her was dark, but she could still make out those ovals attached to deformed bodies. Those bodies seemed more relaxed than before, the ovals softer. She could swear that what before looked so severe was almost like a soft round ball of putty.

The music gradually disappeared into the distance. At first, it washed up softly against the restaurant's foggy windows, before evaporating for good. Someone had turned the lights on, because now Kay could clearly see what was before her. Elmer and Moustache were sitting side by side on the bench facing the counter. Elmer seemed to be grinning, while Moustache twirled that toothpick around in his mouth with enviable skill. The Charbonneaus stood near the washroom door, arm in arm, with an expression that seemed to be a mix of bewilderment and muted pleasure. The boy, standing with some wires dangling from his hands, looked at Kay with a self-satisfied, artful smirk.

Suzette found herself beaming as she faced her audience and tried to catch her breath. She was looking right above everyone's head, just past an adoring crowd that seemed to have multiplied in number quite nicely. Two spotlights went on at the very back, illuminating the two of them for the whole world to see and marvel at. Surely the night nurse would walk over to her window wondering where on earth that light and thunder of applause was coming from! She would retrieve the phone from her purse and frantically text the head nurse at home using that language of abbreviations that serves as the mother tongue of young people these days.

"Honey, I think we can get down from here now…" Kay was still squinting when she turned to Suzette, who clearly inhabited another realm. "The damned high beams on that car in the parking lot are about to burn a hole right through my cornea."

Kay hopped down from the countertop. She summoned the boy over to help her get Suzette down as well. But she could have probably lifted the old lady down on her own — she felt like a giant. As soon as the two were down, everyone in the audience encircled them.

M. Charbonneau cleared his throat for what seemed like an eternity. His vocal cords must have been rusty. "You can really dance, there! Both of you!" Mme. Charbonneau clutched her husband somewhat awkwardly and nodded in agreement.

Elmer scratched his head. "Yup. You gals put on quite a show for us now … quite a show, I say…"

The boy chuckled quietly to himself as he looked at Kay. It seemed like the cat had caught her tongue again. He might as well relish the moment.

"You should ask the boss man if he'll let you put on a show like that every night. Bet it would help business. You know, even some younger dudes would get a kick out of you when you're like that…" The boy mouthed the word "hot" and he pointed to Kay for all the audience to see.

Kay put her hands firmly on her hips. "You little prick, you … you and your little buddies can't even *begin* to imagine what I can do!"

Kay glanced over to her partner. Suzette's eyes sparkled. "Marvellous, *marvellous*!" She took in the little semicircle of fans and friends around her. She had met them only a few hours ago and she hadn't even exchanged a single word with some of them. But she knew them, they knew her and, after what they experienced together this evening, they were connected — all part of something together.

"All right folks, thanks for coming. We better lock up now. Come visit us again, eh." Kay walked over to the cash register. Elmer glanced at Moustache for a second before he spoke to Kay.

"So, you know, you'd have to wait an hour to catch the bus at this time of night. We can give you a lift. Truck's parked right around the corner. No sweat…"

Kay smirked. "Look at that now, we've got a Good Samaritan here tonight!" Moustache slapped Elmer on the back of his head and returned to chewing on his toothpick. "Well, if my dancing partner is up for a little drive and is willing to keep us company, I might just accept your offer."

Suzette felt as though she had just hit the jackpot. At this rate, it would be well past midnight by the time she got back to the home. *Just imagine the face of the night nurse! Everyone is going to hear about this.*

"Holy crap," the boy muttered sarcastically. "You need a chaperone?"

"Listen sweetie, you never know with buddy here what he's really looking for, right?" Kay threw a set of keys to the boy, who barely caught them in time.

Elmer moved up closer to Kay. "No need to think dirty, now. All I want is a tuna melt next time I come … on the house!"

Kay was counting a stack of twenties in the cash register. She responded without looking up. "Better watch out with all that tuna you eat. That mercury won't do you any good!"

Suzette looked up — everyone seemed to be towering around her.

"*Mercury!*" she exclaimed, as though she had struck gold.

Before she knew it, they were all squished up in a rickety pickup truck, shoulder to shoulder in a row, Suzette right in the middle, with Kay on one side and Elmer, clearly in charge behind the wheel, on the other. It looked like Moustache, pushing up against the passenger door, would go flying out any minute. When they pulled out of the lot, that nice young man was untangling earbuds attached to his phone and the Charbonneaus sat behind fogged-up windows in their car. As they turned onto the deserted road, she could see Mr. Moon sitting in that oversized, rich navy-blue wing chair. It looked like he was drinking Campari and soda on ice. But for the first time, she saw that attached to his shiny, corpulent body were the puniest spaghetti legs. He dangled them, like an idle child, over the universe.

I Have Demons

"You like it sweet…" Father Solomon's words formed an observation, not a question, and they came out more sardonic than he had intended. The dour-looking man sat across the antique coffee table. The round table's dimension was small enough for you to feel the other person's breath on your skin after a heavy sigh. He didn't say a word. The thirty-something man with deep-set eyes, pronounced eyebrows and a worn-out face seemed fixated on the last drops of tea, which he stirred methodically, the steel spoon tapping rhythmically against the nearly empty porcelain cup. Steam rose from the teapot as Father Solomon replenished the cup. For a moment, the man vanished in the fog — Earl Grey serving as a protective, piping hot bergamot-scented haze.

***

"*Lamb of God, you take away the sins of the world: have mercy on us. Lamb of God, you take away the sins of the world: have mercy on us. Lamb of God, you take away the sins of the world: grant us peace…*"

The age-old mantra, repeated by few, slid off the walls of the nearly empty, overheated chapel. Most days, Father Solomon was completely alone with the Divine, with only the muffled, but continuous, noise of cars, buses and people scurrying about on their lunch break, beyond the walls. This day he had company. Lifting up the host, he proclaimed mechanically: "Behold the Lamb of God who takes away the sins of the world. Happy are those who are called to His banquet..."

The pasty white host, rising above the altar, blocked out a man fidgeting in the last row. He took off his toque, revealing dishevelled hair, and coughed violently. The woman sitting in the row directly before him turned her head slightly to the side. She wanted to catch a glimpse of this stranger behind her, but surely this wasn't the time. *They say that idle hands are the devil's workshop. But so is frivolous, self-serving curiosity.*

A female voice mingled with a deep male voice, the latter now more pronounced than before.

"Lord, I am not worthy to receive you, but only say the word and my soul shall be healed..."

The host, now transfigured, landed gently on the woman's tongue, the thin bland wafer all but dissolving into the fissures and crevices. The man, a sunken face hiding behind a black beard, walked up with determination to Father Solomon. In a resolute gesture, the man crossed his arms over his chest, with his hands touching each shoulder — an unmistakable sign that he was not prepared to participate in communion, requesting instead a blessing from the priest. He stared at the priest with an eerie severity as Father placed his hand on the man's forehead.

"May God continue His good work in you..."

Mass, after having weaved carefully through readings, psalms and prayers, reached its crescendo during the Eucharist and then wrapped up hastily. Father Solomon hovered over a stubborn green votive candle next to the altar. It just wouldn't be blown out. Inspecting it closely, he was startled when he realized that Mrs. Turner, a woman ever mindful of appearing proper, bundled up in a dark winter coat and wearing a head scarf, was standing next to him, peering with immense curiosity into that obdurate candle too.

"Father, there's a strange man over there. He's not leaving." She almost whispered this to him, gesturing to a blurry figure sitting in the background.

"The Church is full of strange men, Mrs. Turner." Father Solomon blew out another candle. This one conceded defeat without a fight. "As a matter of fact, I heard that once there was this odd man who raised a corpse from the dead, just by talking to it. Fancy that..." Father Solomon's words were laced with sarcasm. The old Mrs. Turner was often too English for her own good.

"Oh, what ever would we do now without the good father's humour and his charitable nature!" Mrs. Turner smiled and adjusted the purse that dangled uncomfortably on her shoulder.

"Only on Tuesdays and Thursdays, I assure you, Mrs. Turner." Father Solomon spoke without a smile. He was conscious of it and knew he ought to soften up a bit. Once, a parishioner even asked him out of concern if he was unwell or just an overall malcontent.

Mrs. Turner clearly wanted to make conversation, but there was something oppressive in the air, and Father Solomon felt impatient today.

"Well then, I'll be off I suppose. Oh, and before I forget, you know I'm in Toronto for the next few days, *Father*. My sister has taken a turn for the worse, I'm afraid..." Mrs. Turner shook her head, but seemed otherwise resigned to the situation.

"I am sorry..." *There, that sounded much more compassionate*, thought Solomon.

"Well, we all knew the time was coming, though you never can really prepare, can you now? Of course, we all like to say we do..." Mrs. Turner paused reflectively.

"Oh, good heavens, I almost forgot. The Widow Barlow would like a pastoral visit. She doesn't expect to come to Mass during the winter — the sidewalks are far too treacherous and she's been ringing City Hall about that each morning." Father Solomon nodded. It was time for him to receive his list of duties.

"Yes, Mrs. Turner." Although he didn't sound soft, he at least came across as obedient.

"And please pray for the McIntyres — their mother is in a home now — she recognizes not a soul, save for her poodle, Yappy. Didn't forget him at all, it seems. I fear we won't be seeing her again ... and Lord knows her family rarely makes an appearance in the house of the risen Lord. They must be otherwise *engaged*..." Mrs. Turner was better than most at sarcasm. Father Solomon wanted to get in a "yes, of course," but Mrs. Turner started up again before he could slide in a response.

"And please don't forget to find out whatever happened to that poor Mrs. Finnegan. I can't get a hold of her for a week now. It's just not like her..." She paused, realizing she had forgotten something, then looked down at her bag.

"Oh, dear me — where *did* my mind go! I all but forgot that I brought you this cherry liqueur. Just to keep you warm at night, Father. Only a sip now, every now and again. We don't want you ending up like Father O'Callaghan, God rest his soul!"

***

"So then, what exactly is it that I can do for you, Mister...?" Father Solomon had to break the silence. It's not so much that the awkwardness of the strange man tapping that spoon against the teacup or turning it round and round on his saucer especially bothered him; it was more that he began to resent spending time on a man who just sat there brooding, instead of introducing himself. The man abruptly stopped stirring his tea and looked the priest directly in the eye.

"Joseph James Etienne Leclair." The long name rolled off the man's tongue slowly and he seemed to be slurring slightly. "But I go by Joseph on Tuesdays..." His slurred speech morphed into a smirk.

"What can I do for you, Mr. Leclair?" Father purposefully shunned the first-name basis, choosing to maintain boundaries. Leclair returned to stirring his tea.

"You probably can't do anything for me, Father *Mister*." He responded with resignation and acidity.

"It's *Solomon*." Father Solomon was beyond pretending that he was unvexed.

"Solomon. Solomon. Solomon." Leclair kept stirring his tea as he slowly repeated the priest's name. "You can't help. You won't help." His words were a stinging accusation.

"*Try me*." Father leaned across the table to Leclair and spoke in a daring, almost threatening tone. He could see that the nails on the man's fingers were chewed all the way back to the cuticles and the creases in his fingers were caked with dirt.

Leclair was silent only briefly before he spoke matter-of-factly. "I have demons." His eyes were fixed firmly on his tea. He stirred and stirred his tea, but it wouldn't cool off; steam kept rising from that cup.

"We all do." Father Solomon spoke, but Leclair glanced at him at first perplexed, then almost insulted. "You're not alone in that," he added.

"*I have demons*." Leclair appeared to be getting angry at being dismissed. He didn't raise his voice, but it became deeper and sterner. "They speak to me all at once so I can't understand a word they're saying. It's like this chorus of garbled voices."

Father Solomon sighed. "And you can't *at all* make out what they're saying to you?"

Leclair huffed and fell back into his chair in frustration. "Isn't that what I just said?" He glared at the priest.

"I suppose..." Father Solomon looked at the window across the room from them, reflecting on what to say next. The red-and-white articulated bus stopped to pick up a handful of shivering passengers across the street, bundled up from head to foot. Cars zoomed by with drivers nestled in warm seats as this dreary mass gathered anxiously by the front door of the bus. *Would I trade places with them?* Father cleared his throat.

"I am supposed to tell you that we can pray about it together and that prayer is powerful. And it *can* be. But I have to ask you if you've ever spoken about this with someone else. Someone who is equipped to truly help you" — he paused, before adding — "in a more worldly sense..."

Leclair pushed his cup of tea away on the table, crossed his arms and glared at the priest.

"You're gonna send me to a shrink, aren't you? Holy fuck! What a useless place. You of all people should know that shrinks can't help with what I have!" Leclair's voice went from a seething low pitch to a frenzied yell. Solomon was startled but knew that he couldn't show it. *Never tell a person in distress to calm down*, he reminded himself, *but do your best to stay calm and level.*

"I can pray with you, but I don't have any special powers..." If Father Solomon was certain of anything at all, it was that he possessed no magical powers and very few gifts. The ability to exorcise demons wasn't one of them, nor would he make a good psychiatrist. Religion was at its worst when it offered a quick fix, especially when faced with the complex problems of the human mind.

Leclair slammed the table with his fist.

"Fuck yes, you do! You *do*! But you won't use them!" Leclair pointed his finger at Father Solomon. If he'd been a few inches closer, his finger would have gone straight into the priest's right eye.

"Mr. Leclair, if you're referring to what I think you're referring to, it does not work the way you presume it does. I'd have to put you in touch with someone at the diocese who performs the ritual. But I'm not convinced that's what you need..."

"Not convinced, eh? Well why don't you put me in touch with a real priest then, *Father*!"

The man was hissing and seething with an anger that made Earl Grey, apparently unable to cool down, seem lukewarm by comparison. Father focused on slow, calm gestures and body language. He bowed his head and interlaced his fingers, resting his hands just above his belt. He took his time before speaking and allowed for an extended moment of silence to wash out the anger and tension from the room. Silence is an underappreciated gift in the world today.

"Would you like to pray with me?" Father Solomon had been searching for his "soft voice" all day and just maybe, he had finally found it. But he was caught off guard when Leclair leapt out of his chair, only to suddenly drop to his knees, directly in front of the priest. He didn't say a word.

"Is there anything specific that is weighing heavy on your heart, Mr. Leclair?" This time it was Leclair who invited silence into the room. He seemed pensive, deep in thought and was fixated on something he saw in the far corner of the room. When he finally spoke, he sounded reluctant.

"My neighbour ... she's dead." He started nodding his head in agreement with his own assessment, even as he continued to look at whatever he saw in the corner.

"Were you close to her?" Father Solomon sensed that she was something more than a neighbour and that he might have to ask the right questions to flesh out the details needed to get a complete picture. Leclair turned to him and seemed to hesitate less.

"She took me in when I got paroled. Nobody else would. She didn't ask questions, didn't worry about my past one bit." Leclair stared off into space and seemed genuinely stunned as he considered what he was saying.

"Unconditional love…" As Father Solomon spoke those two words, he thought about the innumerable times he had heard them or read them. But he couldn't ever remember actually uttering them.

"She got sick. The last month was difficult on her and on me too. She couldn't bathe without help but was too proud to ask me." The frown lines seemed more pronounced on Leclair's face, eyes dark and drained of life. He was about Father Solomon's age, but it was as though the years in the parallel universe that he inhabited were measured differently.

"She had no family?" Leclair just shook his head in response and returned to staring at the corner of the room. It was as though he was at the cinema and some film, screened only for him, was being projected on the wall.

"She would just lie on the chesterfield all day. That was the spot in the apartment that got the most afternoon sun. It was sort of cozy in the winter. She said she was lying on the beach in Cuba. She pretended that I was an attendant at a resort. She had me bring her rum and Cokes. Then I'd just sit there on the floor next to her in the sun and she'd tell me all about these clunky cars from the fifties that roared down the streets in Havana. And about some cab driver she had a fling with once in the back of one of them vehicles…" Leclair's head was still turned towards the wall as Father Solomon smiled and then chuckled quietly to himself.

"Then it became too painful for her to lie on the chesterfield. She became bedridden. Couldn't leave her bedroom…" Leclair glanced briefly at Father Solomon.

"But you were there for her all along. She had *you*." Father Solomon hoped that he sounded comforting but was never really sure.

Leclair sighed and seemed to muster all his strength. He looked straight at the priest.

"Until I killed her." This time silence crept back into the room of its own accord, uninvited. Father Solomon was taken aback. He pushed the teapot out of the way and didn't know why. It was important to remain composed, but who was this man? And how did this get so lurid?

"She was a pharmacist before she retired. She had worked out *exactly* the right potion, spent an afternoon explaining it all to me, told me it was an act of mercy. I told her I was dense, just a boy from the valley who barely finished high school. It was too much for me. *Too damn much.*" Leclair became increasingly agitated. "She didn't care; she told me that I *had* to do this for her. 'Put on your big boy pants, Joseph!'"

"And you did…" Father Solomon didn't really want confirmation and he sounded tentative.

Leclair nodded, looking away from the priest.

Father Solomon took a deep breath and closed his eyes for a moment. "Who have you told about this?"

"Just you. And now I need you to do something for me…" Leclair was looking directly at Father Solomon with a determined expression. "I need you to drive out with me to the valley to bury her ashes. I still own a little plot of land out there — as a kid, whenever I felt jittery, whenever just seeing people made my chest tighten, whenever I felt like I couldn't catch my breath, I would go out there. I need you to go there with me and bury her. Proper rituals and all."

Father Solomon avoided eye contact. Beyond the window, he saw a city worker in a neon vest sprinkling salt on the glistening sidewalk. Every now and then, he put down the bag and blew warm air into his freezing hands. *Someone should give him gloves.* Father Solomon was startled when Leclair sneezed and grabbed a napkin from the table.

"This is not how it's supposed to work..." Father Solomon saw an odd grin materializing on Leclair's face.

"You're telling me?"

The priest looked away and bit his lips as Leclair finally got up from the floor.

"Tomorrow at two o'clock. I can come get you. I know where to find you."

***

The rectory, once home to a community of priests, had five bedrooms. Solomon occupied the one at the end of the hallway and the rest were euphemistically considered guest rooms. The parish rarely received guests these days. Last year, an enthusiastic historian visiting from Brockville stayed in the rectory for a couple of nights — snapping pictures, scribbling notes, collecting memories and recording a day in the life of a parish priest. Father Solomon felt as though he had come to the end of his life and that the only remaining task was to ensure that fragments of his parish and of his personal existence were preserved for posterity. He hadn't even turned forty, yet his life seemed to be one of farewells and departures. Oddly enough, funerals often brought life to the church. Pews were bursting with grandchildren and young couples. Many of the adults followed the rituals, hymns and responses as outside observers — with a mix of bewilderment, distance and the occasional glimmer indicating that something they heard or saw sparked a memory from their childhood.

Solomon sat on his twin bed, with his legs crossed. The radiator under the window was leaking again and it was time to empty the overflowing margarine tub. His room was bland and somewhat clinical, filled with a harsh white light that made the blue walls seem even less inviting. Solomon didn't believe in accumulating things. When the bishop decided to assign him to a different parish, he'd fit everything he owned in this world into a suitcase, a backpack and one small box. The rinky-dink night table, lamp and crucifix above his bed all belonged to the parish, as did the burgundy rotary dial telephone and the plaster Virgin Mary that stood guard over it.

Sometimes Solomon felt it would be better to have the Mother of God turn away when he was sitting in bed in an undershirt eating strawberry Jell-O from a big salad bowl. He never waited long enough for the Jell-O to set properly and it just wasn't the same without a dollop of whipped cream on top, but there was something weirdly comforting about this bachelor's dinner. The bright-red gelatin brought colour to the otherwise uniformly drab, washed-out room.

Solomon was startled when the phone rang. He reached to pick it up on the third ring.

"This is Father Solomon…" He removed the bowl of Jell-O from his lap. This could be something urgent, a request for an anointing perhaps. But within five seconds, he realized exactly what this was about and felt his blood pressure rise.

"No, no … I am afraid there is no lady of the house here. Yes, I am absolutely certain. God bless." He slammed the receiver back on the phone with enough strength that it let out a short ring. Solomon kept his eyes on the night table. *Decisions, decisions...* Then, with a very deliberate motion, he reached for the drawer, pulled out the bottle of cherry liqueur along with a folded flyer from a department store. Solomon took a gulp straight from the bottle. *Sweet Jesus, this thing tastes like cough syrup.* He put down the bottle on the night table with a thud and grimaced as he swallowed hard.

Solomon began flipping through the pages of the flyer. Vacuum cleaners. Towels and bed linens. Blenders. Spring clothing. *Spring clothing?* Women with perfect skin and impeccable figures modelling lingerie and men with chiselled bodies selling underwear. Smiles all around. Solomon absent-mindedly reached for the cherry liqueur and barely noticed as the thick, nauseatingly sweet syrup filled his mouth and set his throat alight. The room felt warmer than before, the mattress softer and the silence was perfection itself.

***

Leclair crouched on a patch of exposed frozen grass by the church wall as he exhaled cigarette smoke. He was fifteen minutes early and Father Solomon had just returned from dropping off documents at the chancery. Ciarán usually took care of the janitorial and maintenance work around the parish and Father Solomon happily gave him a twenty here and a twenty there to complete the endless mundane tasks that normally landed on his plate. But Ciarán had recently found steady work with a master carpenter and would only be able to help out on weekends. The list that Father Solomon had compiled for him remained untouched. *Salt the walkway. Mop up the puddles at the back of the church. Figure out why the light bulb in the sacristy keeps burning out so fast. Be on standby tomorrow from eight to noon for the repairman to come check out the boiler. Vacuum. Dust. Clean the washrooms. New batteries needed for the mic — the Dollar store ones are just fine. And if all that's done, schedule time to finally varnish the pews.* Father Solomon was mindful of the pastoral chores that Mrs. Turner had given him as well. He hadn't managed to check any of them off yet.

Father Solomon walked over to Leclair, who was still crouching and inhaling the residual fumes from all that remained of his cigarette — a stub. Solomon often complained about having no time for pastoral work due to the relentless, random and mundane chores of the world. Yet now, faced with something that demanded profound pastoral skill, he wanted nothing more than to scrub the washroom at the back of the church.

Everything was wrong with what this man was asking him to do. Last night Father Solomon left a message on Ciarán's answering machine, hoping that, as a result of some miracle (perhaps his carpenter boss fell ill?), he might be able to accompany Solomon as he was driven out to some undisclosed location alongside an urn. Ciarán dutifully returned the call. As it turned out, his boss was doing just fine. No miracle today.

"It doesn't sound like a very good idea," Ciarán paused. "I mean you driving out with this man, alone and all..." Static temporarily drowned out Ciarán's voice. "But I'll tell you straight up, Father — if I could, I'd be there with you in a heartbeat. And I'd bring a shiv, just in case."

His own physical safety was not Solomon's only concern. This man was ill, traumatized, and his perception of reality likely warped. A psychiatrist would meet his patient in the safety of his office, with a receptionist seated on the other side of a thin wall. Professionalism dictated clear boundaries and distance. Pastoral work often relied more on responding compassionately while exercising sound judgment. Solomon wasn't certain that he had it in him to do either.

"Hello..." Father Solomon got no reaction from Leclair. "Why don't we sit down for a coffee in the rectory. How about that?" Maybe he could talk this man off the ledge and save himself an unsettling drive out to nowhere.

Leclair didn't have to say anything — he just glared at Father Solomon. He got up and walked over to his pickup truck without another word. *Was he going to just drive away?* He got into his truck, closed the door and Solomon felt hope embrace him, warming him amidst even the biting cold. But the warmth evaporated as soon as Leclair slammed his palm onto the horn again and again, all the while his eyes fixed firmly on Father Solomon, an unyielding stare through an icy windshield.

For some reason, Solomon couldn't remember ever getting into the truck, but there he was, in the passenger seat, watching Leclair gripping the wheel with one hand and tapping his knuckles against his mouth with the other. He hadn't uttered a word, replacing language with non-verbal communication. There was barely any traffic on the 417. Solomon felt uneasy as they passed the high-rises and modest glass towers of Centretown.

Driving past the YMCA on Argyle, Solomon saw himself sitting in the hot tub after disciplined laps in the pool — enjoying the comfort of his accomplishment, especially as his face felt hot and fiery red from exertion. But as the city gave way to suburbia, then the vast greenbelt, followed by just a sprinkling of homes and then mostly farmland and forests, a sense of foreboding settled over the world of daydreams, quickly suffocating it.

All that Solomon knew was that they were driving west, well past Kanata now, but there was no indication from Leclair as to their final destination. Leclair slowed down as they continued along March Road. The odd house, hidden deep within long lots and marked by little else but a mailbox along the side of the road, was eventually replaced by indistinguishable wilderness on either side.

No sooner had they been greeted by a sign welcoming them to Lanark County than Father Solomon lurched forward to the dashboard as Leclair hit the brakes.

"What's the matter?" Father Solomon's perplexed question was too late to elicit a response. Leclair had jumped out of the truck and started furiously kicking the tire.

"Shit!" Leclair's palm seemed to be glued to his forehead as he looked around him, clearly frustrated and confused. Father Solomon decided that it was time to get out of the truck. He opened the passenger door, got out and cautiously moved toward Leclair, staring at him with a look that demanded immediate clarification.

"I don't know where the fuck we are! All right? Happy now?" Leclair glared at Solomon.

Solomon knew he had to compose himself. *Take a deep breath and don't speak until you're centred.* He tried to chip away at a patch of ice on the pavement with his right shoe, kicking its edges with stubborn vigour. *Okay, go for it.*

"You said that you came to this plot of land many times before..." Solomon's words were tinged with exasperated disbelief.

"Yeah, sure. When I was fifteen. I can't believe this. I've gone all foggy in the head again..." Leclair formed a snowball and threw it at the trees, just barely missing the priest.

"Do something! Do something! *Do something!*" Leclair roared, and it wasn't clear if he was yelling at himself or at Father Solomon.

These were the times that required pastoral patience. Solomon knew that he wasn't any good at it.

"Look, do you want to come back another time?" But Leclair just scowled. "We can go back to the rectory — I've got a regional map in the office. Maybe we'll take a look at it and try again next week. How do you feel about that?" Solomon hoped it wasn't too late to close the curtains on this winter gong show.

But all hopes were dashed when Leclair stormed up to Father Solomon and pushed him against the hood of the truck.

As he came within an inch or two of the priest's nose, Leclair glowered at him, clearly seething.

"There's no going back."

Father Solomon was in an awkward pose against the hood of the truck and his back was beginning to ache.

This was a time to stay calm, cool, level-headed. "It's going to get dark soon. We can't do anything after darkness falls..."

Leclair continued looking at Solomon with fierce intensity. He was still holding onto his coat with one hand but wouldn't say anything. After a moment seemingly frozen in time, he finally let Solomon go. Turning his back to the priest, head bowed, he lay down in the middle of the road, on the thin layer of discoloured snow bearing the tire marks of hundreds of cars, and started making what appeared to be a snow angel.

Solomon should have taken the time to compose himself, but instead he hovered over Leclair, looking down on this bizarre spectacle.

"Mr. Leclair, you need to get up!" Leclair didn't respond and appeared to be caught up in a world of his own. "I said get up!" Solomon had lost his patience and gave Leclair a firm kick in his side as he thundered out an order. It felt good, weirdly healing, but none of that lasted more than a split second. He had kicked the proverbial man right when he was down. Wisdom and ethics, shared across religions and across the vast planes of agnosticism and religious indifference, came together to frown collectively on that sort of thing. Everyone agreed it was sacrilege of the highest order.

Leclair winced and then muttered to himself in distress. "We're not going back. We're not going back. We're not going back."

Mantras are meant to centre the soul and mind. But Leclair sounded more like a scratched-up record, the needle held captive by one of the grooves.

Solomon felt anxiety creeping up on him. He felt light-headed, as though he had run a marathon and was struggling hopelessly to catch his breath — or at least to take in enough oxygen to keep his mind and body operational. They had passed the exit to Kemptville and had turned off the main road. If it were up to him, within an hour they would be reassuringly rolling down the more familiar urban terrain of the 417. Instead, they had to push forward, but neither of them knew where.

***

Solomon hated when he did this. He found himself pacing nervously, having to turn and change direction far too often due to the confines of an oppressive space. He felt as though the four walls of the dingy motel room, covered in wooden panels that had absorbed their fair share of tobacco over the years, were trying much too hard to feel like a cozy forest cabin. It wasn't working. They were conspiring to asphyxiate him.

An hour earlier, he and the man had been on the edge of a small town. Leclair was silent as Father Solomon gave him directions to the only place in the area he'd visited before: Almonte. Mill Street, a cheerful little strip during the summer months, was deserted as the sun began its descent on this frigid evening in March. Leclair turned his head and blew cigarette smoke towards the street. He didn't seem to think he had any responsibility in helping Solomon find lodging for the night. Leclair refused to turn back, had no viable plan to move forward and appeared to have retreated into himself.

Eerie circus music seemed to linger above the town — the type that only a carnival clown would like: the thin, unconvincing layer of childlike bliss that serves to conceal at best profound sadness and at worst something sinister not far below. *A circus on a weeknight in early March?* Solomon felt disoriented.

One of the antique shops was still open and he could see an older woman perched on a stool behind the till, reading a book.

"Wait for me here." Solomon sounded as though he were instructing a child. Leclair's eyes seemed glazed over, uninterested in his surroundings or the priest. "I'll be as quick as I can."

Solomon kept an eye on Leclair as he perused the store, looking for something small and inexpensive to buy in exchange for the woman's help finding lodging. Solomon saw the world and human interaction as a web of mutually beneficial transactions. The woman needed business; he needed local information. They could help each other without one side doing the other a favour. Nobody would feel vulnerable.

Leclair was still standing outside the store facing the street, shifting his weight from one foot to another, as though he had to use the washroom. Deep down, Solomon quietly hoped that the next time he turned around, Leclair would be gone — maybe he would climb back into his truck and drive away. Being stranded alone sounded so good now. Solomon would spend a quiet night in Almonte and then find his way back to the city the next morning, one way or another. It would be a relief. *But would it really?* Leclair looked far more pathetic than menacing. He didn't need to pee. He was clearly freezing out on Mill Street.

The aroma of coffee lingered in the shop, combined with the warm, signature smell that emanates from things of the past: ornate oak cabinets and side tables, mechanical typewriters, books, postcards, old paper bills, radios and telephones. The marble cherubim and an eclectic mix of mismatched Royal Albert cups and saucers tempered the homey atmosphere with the cool remnants of class. You would need the patience of an oyster to painstakingly find, over years and years of searching, enough matching cups and saucers to create a complete set. In the quietest corner of the shop sat a record player and a tower of records. There was something soothing about obsolete technology; it lost that edge of functionality, of being in demand and of being indispensable. It was harmless and still.

"That poor, poor man…" The woman behind the counter let her thick-rimmed glasses slide down to the middle of her nose as she peeked out the door. "One can't help but wonder how on earth the homeless make it out all the way here and what they hope to find…"

Solomon absent-mindedly picked up a cup and saucer adorned with the prairie lily and walked over to the counter.

"No, madam. As a matter of fact, he is with me." The woman caught a glimpse of Solomon's clerical collar and her facial muscles seemed to go soft.

"Reverend!" she exclaimed with an enthusiastic smile. "Are you from around here? I don't believe I've seen you before." She carefully took the cup and saucer from Solomon's hands, inspecting it lovingly from every angle. "Well now, look what you've found — isn't it just lovely, Reverend!" She began scraping the handwritten five-dollar price tag off the inside of the cup.

"I am Father Solomon, from Ottawa…" Solomon's voice trailed off as the woman stopped her scraping and as her facial muscles tensed up. She put the cup and saucer on the counter. Her glasses slid to the very tip of her nose as she inspected Solomon from head to toe and then from toe to head. Her face softened and she returned to her scraping of the intransigent price tag.

"I'm Baptist." *Scrape, scrape.* "But we're very tolerant around these parts. Very tolerant of all kinds," she added without looking up.

Solomon found the air heavy. The smell of old books, oak furniture and knick-knacks was no longer warm and familiar. It had become stuffy and oppressive. He thought he could still hear traces of that circus music creeping into the shop. It seemed obnoxious, obscene.

"May I ask you a question, madam?" Solomon wasn't sure if it was appropriate to disturb her amidst her scraping. She didn't look up and she didn't stop.

"Well of course. We don't bite…"

"My friend and I are looking for a room." He glanced at Leclair, who huddled over his lighter as he lit up another cigarette. This time, the woman behind the counter looked up with a poker face. Father Solomon forced out a short cough. "More of an acquaintance, actually. We just need something economical for the night…" His voice trailed off again. The woman made him nervous. One moment she seemed to be a kindly shop owner, the next he felt like a student entering the hallowed offices of a stern headmistress.

"*Economical*, of course…" The shop owner's hands sped up as she wrapped the china in tissue paper. "There are a couple of places right out of town that should suit you and the gentleman outside." She took Solomon's five and quickly placed it in the till. "They're barely a ten-minute drive from here. You should have no trouble finding them." A faint smile returned to her face. Solomon nodded and said a barely audible thank you as he turned towards the door.

"Is there any chance I can interest you in a Bible?" She fiddled with her eye glasses in her hands as Solomon reached for the door. "I have a beautiful hardcover King James Version, gilded page edges." She gave Solomon a wide smile, baring her teeth. "Some good reading for you while you enjoy your next tea from that gem of a cup!"

***

Leclair was in bad shape. Solomon had found them adjacent rooms at a tired motel on the edge of town — the Lanark Solstice Inn. But he hadn't had a chance to check out his room. No sooner had they arrived than Leclair grabbed one set of keys from Solomon's hand, opened the door and shut himself in the bathroom.

"Is everything all right?" Father Solomon stood outside the door and heard the sound of water spraying from the shower, bouncing off the porcelain tub. No response.

"Mr. Leclair, are you all right?" Father Solomon slowly opened the door and saw Leclair, naked, sitting under the shower head in the bathtub, with hot water pouring on him. A thick cloud of steam enveloped the small bathroom; the white and turquoise tiles glistened.

"Pardon me, I didn't mean to intrude..." Solomon looked away feeling awkward. He instinctively turned around, about to exit the bathroom as quickly as possible. Leclair made no eye contact; he continued to stare at the moist tiles across from him. Motionless.

"If I don't take the pills, they say I'm not myself. If I *do* take the pills, I'm lost in a haze so deep that my brain feels like a milky mush." Leclair rubbed all ten fingers over the top of his scalp, pushing his dark drenched hair away from his forehead. He tilted his head back, let the shower fill his mouth with water and then spat it out.

"It's a lose-lose situation. I'm cursed."

Solomon determined that Leclair's decision to talk signalled that he was comfortable with him staying. When someone said they were cursed, Solomon often viewed the declaration as self-pity. He was notoriously impatient with people who wallowed in it. He found it too easy, and taking the easy way out, frivolous. But this was different. Leclair was tormented and had no road map to guide him out of his agony. Water had splashed across much of the bathroom floor and Solomon saw that Leclair's clothes, which lay in a deflated pile next to the tub, were getting wet too. He picked up the pile, the socks on top completely soaked, opened the bathroom door and dropped them on the other side. Leclair's eyes followed the pile as it was carried out, as the door opened and closed, without making eye contact with the priest. Solomon sat down on the floor in the space between the sink and tub, directly parallel to Leclair, and crossed his legs. He closed his eyes for an extended moment, inhaled and exhaled before speaking.

"Tell me about your neighbour, when she was still well..." Solomon determined that he didn't need to look at Leclair directly. He stared ahead at the towel rack in front of him, and Leclair kept his eyes on the tiled wall, where drops of condensation grew and grew until they could hang on to the smooth, slippery surface no longer and trickled all the way down. The sound of the water spraying from the shower, with occasional stray droplets landing on Solomon's forehead, was like soft, soothing background music — monotone, predictable, safe.

From the corner of his eye, Solomon thought he saw Leclair smile faintly.

"When I was like this, she never gave me booze, even when she'd have sherry in the afternoon herself. She sat in a wing chair, layed back and rested her feet on a stool. Her body was like this blob, all comfy. I never knew where her breasts ended and where her belly began. She wasn't really hot shit.

But it didn't matter how she looked — it's not as if we were screwing or anything. I was usually glued to some afternoon garbage on cable. And she just sipped away and buried herself in a copy of *Reader's Digest* before dozing off. She felt bad for me. Once, she prepared a Shirley Temple but said I can't ever let my old cellmates and prison buddies know. She said a Shirley Temple isn't a good look for a guy like me." Leclair folded his arms and chuckled.

"Nor for me..." For the first time in longer than he could remember, Solomon felt genuinely amused. A smirk settled on his face — that youthful, innocuously mischievous smirk that often fades with time. Although his simper receded almost as quickly as it had come, he found himself mostly at ease. He started slowly.

"You know, I can't pretend to know what you're experiencing. But what you told me about yesterday — what you say you had to do..." Father paused, taking in a gulp of the humid air as he inhaled. The air tasted mildly of citrus as it settled on his tongue. *Shampoo?*

"You were in a really tough spot and I don't know what I would have done in your place. But when we examine our conscience, it's the intention and motive that counts the most."

Leclair's mood darkened. "She was all but begging me. A woman who opened her home to a wreck who had shit-all to show for his thirty-five years on this earth. Except for a conviction." A long paused followed and both seemed content to sit in the warm, dewy silence. Eventually Leclair chuckled to himself quietly and Solomon glanced at him.

"Hey, does this count as a confession? Am I good, *Father*?"

Solomon slowly got up from the bathroom floor. The hot air seemed to have zapped him of his energy and he felt dizzy. He opened the bathroom door a crack, but the crisp, cool air that snuck in proved decidedly unwelcome. He turned to look at Leclair, who had finally shut the water off and was rubbing his eyes.

"Put your clothes on. I'm going to get us something to eat."

***

Every fifteen seconds or so, a car or truck zoomed by Solomon, who felt increasingly out of place walking along the side of a road not meant for pedestrians. *If it isn't the biting wind, a minivan will put me out of my misery today.* He hadn't realized how tattered he'd looked until he got back to his own motel room after dealing with Leclair. He'd seen himself in the long mirror hanging on the bathroom door. His navy-blue pants looked slightly purple, discoloured from years of repeated washes, wear and tear, and the sun. Road salt was diligently eating away at the leather on his cracked, beat-up shoes, and even his black clerical shirt seemed to be fading. Solomon didn't look unkempt as such. He just seemed worn — like the old man who makes the effort of dressing up properly every weekday in a tired fifty-year-old suit, smelling mildly of mothballs, the remnants of decades-old cigar smoke absorbed deep into the fabric and the residual whiff of cheap drugstore cologne.

The walk to the nearest convenience store was proving more treacherous than Solomon had thought it would be. In the dark of a cold March night, he was nothing more than a shadowy figure without a face, dressed in nondescript, gloomy clothing, making his way down the narrow strip of icy gravel that ran between the pavement and a ditch along the length of the road. Solomon turned back for a moment to size up the next vehicle to hurtle by him. It was better to know what was coming, instead of being startled. He noticed that it must be a truck: orange lights piercing the darkness above the windshield and that deep, mature rumble that declares with confidence that you're not dealing with some namby-pamby hatchback.

The truck seemed to be slowing down as it approached him. Solomon kept walking and didn't look back. By the time it reached him, the truck must have been going at just twenty kilometres per hour or less, coming to a complete stop about ten metres up the road. *What did he want? Did he need help?* Solomon felt apprehension gather in him as he walked by the side of the truck. The passenger door flung open as he got close and he could hear a voice and the crackle of a two-way radio. As he reached the passenger door, he glanced inside as quickly as possible, hoping not to be noticed. He really just wanted to slink by. No such luck.

"Holy cow, it's minus twenty-two with the wind chill, now. You're gonna freeze your butt right off in no time!" The plump woman in a jean jacket looked down on Solomon with a big smile, then moved her chewing gum around to a more convenient location in her mouth. Her bleached blonde hair was short and dull, with only a few random spikes of gel on the top giving it some life and texture. But it was the oversized square fuchsia clip-ons covering each earlobe that caught Solomon's attention.

Solomon smiled sheepishly and bowed his head slightly.

"It's really not too bad, madam." It *was* bad — every few minutes Solomon had to cover his ears because he could barely feel them anymore. He realized when he spoke that his facial muscles were frozen too and he felt as though he was slurring.

"Well where ya headed?" The woman's smile remained constant.

"Oh, just a short way down the road, to a convenience store. I was told it's a quick walk…" The woman raised her eyebrows.

"I'd say you got yourself some bad info there, buddy!" She scratched her head and turned towards the windshield, squinting. "Oh yeah. You're lookin' at a good two kilometres."

Solomon didn't remember getting in her truck, but there he was, perched higher above the road than he'd ever been, with almost a bird's-eye view of the terrain. His glance caught a plastic toy Smurfette on the dashboard, complete with exaggerated lashes, white shoes and flowing blonde hair.

"It's no trouble at all, bud. I was gonna get myself a pack of smokes and some ginger ale anyway. Don't matter where I get it. We'll check out the little corner shop together, eh?"

Solomon folded his hands in his lap and glanced over to the woman. "Thank you."

"Sheila." She extended her right hand, gripping the wheel with the left. Solomon really wished she would just focus on the road. He hesitated for a brief moment before shaking her hand.

"Solomon."

Sheila's smile filled not only her face, but seemingly the whole cabin.

"Love it! My husband's little brother is called Solomon. Sweetest guy on earth!"

Solomon felt she was giving him an opportunity to ask a polite question.

"What does your husband do, Sheila?" It seemed appropriate to ask. She chuckled before responding.

"Oh, dear ... *well*, Todd is mostly torturing himself about not being enough of a man."

Solomon felt a sense of worry build in his stomach. Did he just unwittingly stroll into a minefield?

"He's a stay-at-home dad, you see, ever since an accident made him useless in construction. He tried out working behind a desk answering calls at the local clinic, but that sure didn't turn out to be his thing." Sheila didn't sound bitter and there was no edge to her tone. She was stating incontrovertible facts.

"How old are your kids?" Solomon hoped that he wasn't prying. Again, the information she shared seemed to invite the question.

"Our son's fifteen and let me tell you, that kid's sweet as pie! But he needs a little extra help you know. And Todd turned out to be a grade-A caregiver. I'm gone Monday to Friday, on the road sometimes eight hundred kilometres away. But you should see him throw together a banquet each night at the kitchen table. God, he has my son under a spell whenever he's at work in the kitchen. That kid just sits there focusing on him chopping, mixing, kneading, frying like there's nothing else going on in the whole wide world. Oh, he just *loves* the rhythm of onions being diced on the wooden cutting board at my husband's breakneck speed. Yeah, he gets a real kick out of it. Sometimes my husband slows down, just to see if the kid's paying attention. And is he ever! He gets all pissed off and frustrated — God, it's cute — and only calms down when my husband picks up the speed again..." Sheila wasn't really talking to Solomon; she was describing a scene back home to herself, smiling with satisfaction, wrapped up in the image of home.

"It sounds to me that your husband is quite the man, doing a real man's work." Solomon glanced over to Sheila, who seemed amused.

"You're kinda different, aren't you?" She chuckled. "I guess you're a priest or something?"

"Yes, something…" Solomon smiled with boyish mischief. He didn't think he was capable of that. And if he still was, was it even a good look for him? He refocused himself. "Almost anyone with two arms and two legs can pour cement, replace a roof or carry a couch down a flight of stairs. Yes, all of that takes skill and physical strength and manpower. It's important work; I would not doubt that for a moment..." Solomon paused and rubbed the palm of his hand. "But Todd is working day in and day out on a parallel plane, if that makes any sense. The product of his labour is not as tactile or as visible, in a physical sense, as newly installed drywall or resurfaced asphalt. It may be invisible to the naked eye, at least at first glance. But it's there and it's real. He's building the Kingdom with nothing but his bare hands. In fact, I think that for your son at least, the kingdom is already here."

Sheila didn't respond at first, and her smile was barely visible now. But she seemed to be nodding to herself, until she turned to Solomon.

"Nice sermon, bud."

Solomon felt self-conscious. Most people, himself included, hated preachiness, especially when laced with morally superior platitudes.

"Sorry," he muttered.

Sheila's eyes opened wide in surprise. "No, no! It was good. *Very* good!" She let out a deep, fulsome laugh, followed by a satisfied sigh. "Haven't been to church in ages, so what can I say? I guess you brought church to me. Dammit, you're a sneaky little one, aren't ya now?"

***

It turned out that Sheila was spending the night at the Lanark Solstice Inn too. She explained that Wednesday night was always a special treat. Monday and Tuesday, she parked her truck in a quiet spot somewhere and slept in the vehicle. She was lucky if she found a truck stop nearby with a shower and proper facilities. Wednesday, though, she had her routine. She would check into a local motel, soak in the tub, order in some Chinese and watch sitcoms until she fell asleep on the plush queen-size bed. She woke up with a bounce in her step on Thursday and it kept her going until she got home on Friday afternoon.

When they got back to the motel, Solomon found Leclair sitting on the end of the bed in just his underwear and T-shirt staring at the television, a mere metre or two from the box. He seemed to be thoroughly wrapped up in his own world, and Solomon couldn't tell if he was registering anything at all of what was on. Private investigator Thomas Magnum drove down the lush palm tree–lined streets of Oahu, with haughty Higgins lurking around the grand beachfront estate, trying his absolute best to keep the wayward detective on the straight and narrow, inserting that requisite dose of misery that makes life *life*.

Looking at the contents of his brown paper bag, Solomon had to admit that this was hardly a banquet of heavenly proportions — a bag of white bread, peanut butter, processed cheese spread in a glass jar, two apples, a carton of milk. He hadn't had much to work with at the store.

Leclair took no notice of Solomon. He continued to stare at the television — one moment blankly, the next moment as though something he saw was going to suck him right in through the screen. That's how Solomon found him during a laundry detergent commercial. Soiled clothing spun and spun in a machine until a pleasant little bell went off. Then a gorgeous woman with blinding white teeth held up an immaculate white T-shirt, her face melting away in a joy so sublime that one would have thought it was none other than the Holy Mother who materialized miraculously from the soapsuds. Leclair leaned forward as though something was beckoning him. *What was he seeing?*

"I am sure you're hungry by now…"

No answer.

"Do you prefer peanut butter or the cheese spread?" Solomon held up each, the peanut butter in his right hand, the cheese spread in his left. He felt like *he* was in the commercial now.

Leclair didn't acknowledge him.

"Or would you like to try both? There's nothing wrong with doing that either. Joseph?"

Leclair didn't look directly at Solomon, but he did move his head for the first time and looked towards him. Maybe the spell was breaking. Solomon had him sit on the side of the double bed, facing the other one parallel to it. He moved the telephone and notepad to the corner of the night table and used a plastic knife from the store to spread peanut butter on one slice of bread and cheese on the other. He handed both to Leclair. Neither uttered a word. There would have been plenty to talk about, but somehow this didn't seem like the right time. Leclair seemed deflated but calm as he bit into the piece with the peanut butter first. Solomon hunched forward in the tight space between the two beds, directly across from Leclair, opened the carton of milk and passed it over the narrow carpeted valley to the taciturn man across from him. Leclair seemed transfixed by something on the carton, something that Solomon simply could not see. Then, as if woken from this hypnosis, Leclair chugged it back.

***

Solomon, Leclair and Sheila each lay in their own rooms that night at the Lanark Solstice Inn. The winds had died down and light snow danced its way to the ground — unhurried, sauntering through the air. Sheila was in the room next to Solomon. He could hear her speaking softly on the phone —

murmurs, fragments of words. She had invited him to join her for Chinese delivery in her room and told him that she really wanted to meet his friend too.

"I'm afraid he's … shy. He can get very anxious around new people." Sheila gave Solomon a knowing look. She didn't press the issue further.

The cool-blue light from the motel's sign streamed in through the crack in the curtains. Solomon had forgotten how quiet the country could be at night. Sheila had hung up the phone, the passengers in the cars that roared down the road only a few hours before had all arrived home safely and the television box sitting in each room contemplated its existence in silence.

＊

They were all there; each one of them soaking blissfully in that grand pool of warm, foaming water. Steam lifted from the surface, carrying their lilting voices into the wintry forests that surrounded them. Solomon was surprisingly comfortable in the plush white bathrobe as he stood at the edge of the water, looking in. Only his feet were getting cold. A thin layer of ice on the walkway cracked under his weight.

The waters before him were emerald, lush and soft, and the bathers seemed inexplicably transfigured. It's not that their bodies had changed as such. From a strictly physical perspective, Leclair bore deep scars. The middle-aged woman next to him had a distended abdomen that broke the surface of the water. She held a cocktail in her hand and her tan signalled to the world that she had just returned from a beach holiday. The old Mrs. Turner from weekday Mass and her sister, adorned in a homemade turban, both had puckered necks and arms. The agile lady from the antique shop looked surprisingly frail without her clothes on. Sheila's well-worn and ill-fitting bathing suit appeared liable to burst open at a moment's notice and her husband's chest was covered in tattoos acquired during his youth — ones he now undoubtedly regretted. And in between these portly parents sat a boy who seemed far too fragile for his age.

The bathers all bore the unmistakable marks of an unforgiving life. There was hardly a bath in this world or the next that could ever wash away the telltale signs of suffering that transcended all languages, peoples and nations. Yet Solomon could see that this motley group had been transfigured in a real way, though it was next to impossible for him to rationalize what he was witnessing. It was something akin to people who had every reason in the world to brood, agonize, rue or mourn instead of sitting in perfect tranquility, chatting with ease, even with strangers.

Small frozen pellets with sharp edges fell from the sky, pricking Solomon's skin. His toes were slowly going numb. Time to enter the water. Should he remove the robe? The pellets seemed to be growing in size. At first they simply fell on him, but increasingly, it felt as though they were being hurled. The pellets transformed themselves into round silver pieces, smooth on the surface, but startling and painful when they hit Solomon between his eyes.

The icy forest dissolved into dated prefabricated wood panels on four walls and there was no sign of water. As his eyes focused, Solomon could see Leclair dressed in his winter coat and toque, leaning on the dresser across from the bed, throwing quarters at him. For the first time, a grin — a demented grin — seemed painted across Leclair's face.

"What on earth is your problem *now*?" Solomon picked up a quarter and hurled it back at Leclair, hitting the television screen instead. Everything about Leclair seemed exaggerated — his voice, his body language, how he ducked at the sight of the incoming coin.

"But, *Father*, you of all people gotta know that idle hands are the devil's workshop, right?"

Leclair's teasing tone suddenly gave way to genuine surprise as he inspected a quarter in the palm of his hands. "Oh, *shit* — they made Queen E look older again..." Leclair mumbled something as he walked over to Solomon, sitting up in the bed, thoroughly unamused. He put the coin under Solomon's nose. Father glared.

"A penny for your thoughts?" Leclair attempted a terrible impersonation of an English accent before suddenly pulling the covers off of Solomon's bed. He hunched over and held his stomach as he burst out in laughter — whether it was genuine or forced was unclear — at the sight of Father Solomon exposed in his underwear.

With slow, deliberate, seething movements, Father Solomon got out of bed and stood up straight, a couple of inches from Leclair. He spoke with cold articulation.

"Go grab the urn, warm up your truck and wait for me *quietly* in the vehicle." Leclair seemed taken aback by the paternalistic, irritated tone. Father Solomon sounded like a school teacher scolding a bratty kid.

"Well, fuck me..." Leclair kicked the television stand.

As Leclair stormed out, he all but knocked over Sheila, who had materialized outside the door. An unlit cigarette hung limply from the side of her mouth. She took a thorough look — up and down — at the almost-naked Solomon before feigning modesty and turning her back to him.

"So your buddy here ... interesting fella, eh?" Her voice trailed off as she lit her cigarette. "I helped him convince the receptionist that it was okay to give us the key to your room."

She glanced back at Solomon, who was clumsily putting on his pants, nearly tripping over himself.

"Sorry 'bout that. He said you guys were gonna be late to something important. It couldn't wait, he said."

Solomon nodded his head slightly and sighed as he stared aimlessly at the carpet.

"Hey, so how 'bout we have a quick breakfast?" She stopped to puff smoke in the direction of the cars on the road. "It's free. Comes with the price of the room."

As Sheila closed the door behind her and Leclair retreated into his truck, the room became mercifully quiet. Solomon splashed lukewarm water on his face and rubbed his eyes before deciding on a quick shower. The water spraying from the showerhead was scalding and Solomon struggled to set it to a more comfortable temperature. He unwrapped the little square of soap provided by the motel. It was as hard as a rock and its scent was faded. He still didn't understand what he was doing here. Or more precisely, he understood perfectly well what he was being asked to do but began to question whether he was losing his mind to even go along with it. All he knew was that this unsettled, guilt-ridden man claimed to have poisoned his neighbour, at her request no less, and needed a priest to bury her ashes and somehow offer him absolution. But could he? He had all the official lines down pat. God's salvific mercy and forgiveness was mediated through *His* Church. It wasn't so much that he was invested with special powers, but more that as Leclair's confessor, as it were, he could serve as a real, tactile conduit of God's healing grace. *What a wretched vehicle he is, though. God's forgiveness knows no bounds, it's freely available to all and it defies human language and thought.* Yet that intricate web of laws, traditions and revelation, at times opaque — like the steamed-up bathroom mirror in which Solomon could no longer see his own face — so effectively curtailed the infinite.

***

Breakfast at the Lanark Solstice Inn was something of a bad joke. Granola bars and sticky pre-packaged muffins — ones that never managed to go dry — lay in an unceremonious pile at the far end of the check-in counter in the lobby. Solomon decided to go with a pack of instant oatmeal, while Leclair hummed and rubbed his head through his toque.

Sheila slipped a couple of granola bars into her jean jacket as soon as the receptionist retreated into the office behind the lobby. "Well, looks like I've got a long drive ahead of me today..."

Solomon could feel that Sheila wanted to be asked where she was going. He pushed the clumpy oatmeal in the plastic bowl back and forth with his spoon. *It could use more water.*

"First stop: Cornwall. Then over to the States. Massena, Ogdensburg, Watertown. Gotta get it all in before sundown." Sheila took a sip of her coffee through the hole in the plastic lid. "God, it's that bridge I hate..." Both Solomon and Leclair stopped eating and had an almost identically confounded look.

"It's so damn high, hanging way above the Saint Lawrence. Christ, it's narrow too. For a second you almost think it's taking you to the on-ramp of the highway to heaven or something." She chuckled to herself. "Except on the other side there's no angel waiting for you. Not even Michael Landon, that hunk. All you'll find in Massena is a boring mall and a JC Penney with some bargain-hunting Canadians milling about. God, the rust's just eating away at the whole damn place."

***

After Sheila drove off, Leclair had three cups of coffee in rapid succession. He filled the bottom third of his paper cup with sugar, followed by two thirds with coffee. No creamer. When the cup was nearly empty, he used his fingers to make sure none of the undissolved sugar at the bottom went to waste. Solomon didn't realize that he had been glaring at him with a combination of disgust and disapproval until Leclair looked up from his cup. "What's it to you, eh?"

They drove out to a wooded area in complete silence. It would have been a thoroughly uncomfortable silence had Solomon not felt so exhausted. He was mentally worn out. Just as he thought he would somehow bring himself to speak, he realized that forming a coherent sentence took far too much effort. He put his hand on the urn that bounced around between the two seats. He realized the biggest problem: a space dominated by absence, devoid of human words, could be sacred, so long as it was filled with unspoken content. But with his eyes glazing over as they settled on the endless white outside — the frozen ground, the milky sky — his mind sank in a blank, thoughtless sea.

It was simply impossible to keep up with Leclair. He was a man on a mission, hell-bent, with a fire in his belly as he pushed branches out of his way and trudged through the forest. Solomon, struggling to keep up with the pace, was too out of breath to talk.

The brisk pace of this forced hike woke him up.

"We are going to have a hell of a time with the soil — it's still frozen." Solomon paused, waiting for a response from Leclair, but none was forthcoming. He didn't even look back.

Solomon stopped, standing still on a stump that peeked out from the snow.

"Are you certain that we're going the right way? I don't see how you can know. It's all the same everywhere you look. An endless winter maze." A branch, like a gnarly, arthritic finger poking, jabbing at his body, got caught in his coat, and Solomon felt his irritation rise.

This time Leclair stopped. He looked back with a determined expression but did not respond. A moment later, he continued walking and picked up his pace.

It must have been around minus five outside, but Solomon was perspiring under his heavy pea coat. The back of his shirt was damp. He hated the sensation.

After another ten minutes or so, the two arrived at a small nondescript clearing in the middle of the woods. Solomon couldn't see anything that set it apart from the monotonous scenery that surrounded them.

"This is it?" At first, Solomon sounded surprised. It quickly transformed into sarcasm. "So then *this* is that plot of land that you recall so fondly from your youth? That hallowed land from the good old days?"

Leclair, turned the other way, did not answer.

"Mr. Leclair, please will you respond? I have come out all this way with you, blown my monthly discretionary budget on that motel and put up with you and your every whim for nearly twenty-four hours. Do you think that maybe I have earned a response from you?" Solomon's face turned red and he wanted nothing more than to take a nice heavy branch and knock Leclair over the back of his head.

Leclair turned around slowly, with the urn in his hands. His hell-bent determination seemed to have given way to a quiet gloom. He was almost inaudible.

"Start digging ... *please.*"

Solomon let out a sigh of exasperation before pushing his shovel through the snow and into the ground. Leclair fell to his knees and started frantically scraping away snow with his hands. Solomon realized that Leclair was becoming increasingly troubled. During the novitiate, he never learned what to do in situations like this, and even a decade of experience in pastoral ministry had not really prepared him.

Father Solomon knew the liturgy better than most and could follow the script in front of him to the letter. For the most part, he took comfort knowing that even meeting with mourning families was a scripted process in most cases. With few exceptions, he knew what was expected of him, and the grieving loved ones knew what they could expect from their priest. This time, he had strayed far off the path and had nothing to guide him. He didn't really know if he did it for Leclair or for himself, but he quietly recited a verse as he tried to press the shovel into the frozen ground.

"There are many rooms in my Father's house; if there were not, I should have told you. I am going now to prepare a place for you, and after I have gone and prepared you a place, I shall return to take you with me; so that where I am you may be too..."

Solomon's voice trailed off as he realized how little progress he was making, despite his best efforts. The shovel barely scraped two or three inches of earth from the surface.

Leclair sat back on the snow next to the exposed dirt and seemed to be contemplating something.

"Did you say that for me too?" He made eye contact with Solomon briefly.

"It applies to each and every one of us." Solomon sounded brusque as he focused on making the hole big enough to at least reach the top of the urn. Thankfully, it was a small unadorned rectangular box. He had some way to go, but the task no longer seemed unfeasible. He pushed the shovel into the ground and put all his weight on the handle. He could see Leclair from the corner of his eye, sitting quietly and looking away towards the trees.

"Let us find shelter and solace in Your compassion as we return the ashes of our sister to the earth. Grant her a place of peace where the world of dust and ashes has no dominion."

Leclair was staring intently at the urn. The grave was now deep enough to at least cover it, though admittedly it would rest a mere inch or so below the surface of the forest. Solomon picked up the urn and handed it to Leclair, motioning for him to place it in the grave. Leclair got on his knees and placed the urn into the ground with what appeared to be exaggerated care, as though he were handling delicate porcelain.

"*Eternal rest grant unto her, O Lord...*" Father Solomon paused and waited a moment for Leclair to say the scripted response. When he remained silent and withdrawn, Father Solomon concluded. "*And let perpetual light shine upon her.*"

Leclair got up and walked a few feet away from the grave. Suddenly, he turned to Solomon and spoke with a blank expression and monotone voice.

"And upon *me* as well." Leclair produced a pocket knife, swallowed hard, and a look of alarm, combined with a streak of determination, settled on his face. Solomon was momentarily startled, but some instinctive force made him take a few steps towards Leclair.

"What are you doing?" Solomon moved closer to Leclair who remained frozen, now with an expression of impending doom. "Joseph?"

Leclair had slunk away into a different world and his body was as inanimate as a plaster statue. Solomon moved closer to him, slowly, without sudden motions. Leclair seemed to be staring right beyond him, or through him, but it wasn't at all clear what had him so fixated. The knife was firmly in his grip by his left side. His white knuckles protruded from his hand, as his grip formed an uncompromising fist around the knife.

It seemed impossible at this point to take it from him easily. So without the careful forethought that normally brought Solomon comfort, he instinctively came up close to

Leclair from the left, and with one sudden and deliberate swoop, he used all his force to give Leclair a vigorous shove. First surprise, then red rage, settled on Leclair's face as he stumbled and tried to regain his balance. Before he could react, Solomon gave him one final shove. As he stumbled and fell, Solomon reached for the knife. At first, he noticed nothing but warm liquid melting his frostbitten hands. The dizzying pain, laced with terror, came moments later when Solomon noticed that he had all but skewered his hand with the knife that remained firmly in Leclair's grasp.

Letting out a primal roar, Leclair kicked Solomon in the chin. The priest fell on his back and lay there as blood pooled next to his hand in the snow. Disoriented, he no longer knew who he was — or why he was. His eyes were fixed on the milky sky above, and he felt as though his spirit had passed into that murky no man's land between wakefulness and sleep.

In his daze, through the corner of his eye, he noticed that strange figure in burgundy plaid pacing nearby. It came into clearer focus as it hovered above him. Solomon groaned. He became conscious of Leclair muttering as he wrapped what appeared to be his scarf around Solomon's bleeding hand and tightened it.

"Shit!" Leclair took off his toque and ran his fingers through his hair. "I didn't want that to happen to you." He got up, walked over to a tree and rammed the knife into the bark. Solomon slowly sat up and looked at his hand. Blood stained the fabric of the grey scarf. Leclair turned around and, within a moment, loomed over Solomon.

"You've done your part. Now let me finish what needs to be finished, for fuck's sake!"

Silence filled the clearing in the forest for several drawn-out moments, before Solomon cleared his throat and answered.

"It's already done. This heavy burden is no longer yours alone to bear."

Leclair smirked, shook his head and then scoffed.

"It's done when I don't have to feel anymore ... when it's silent and dark and when that chorus finishes its song." He kicked some snow towards the shallow grave and cursed the priest. Solomon could see him retreat to the furthest corner of the clearing and squat down, facing the forest. He let his head hang as he exhaled and spoke, perhaps more to himself than to the priest.

"I fell asleep once, as a kid, in an area just like this. I'm thinking it was around early spring and the last real snowfall cooled me as I just lay there. The skin on my face was on fire something godawful. Swollen, red, throbbing and all. Every flake of snow slowly put out that fire and I just floated away. But I swear I could hear faint steps in the snow coming up towards me. I hadn't gone crazy or anything. These were real fuckin' steps. True, they were soft and all, but real. Careful, distant, getting closer. And then warm moisture on my face. It tickled a little, but in a real good way. It was soft and warm, like a kiss. I thought it was a girl and then I lay there telling myself, hey, I don't mind that one bit now, keep it comin'." Leclair paused and glanced back at Solomon. "Oh, right, you wouldn't know, eh?"

Solomon grinned.

"But that warm, sweet girl kissing me in the snow had some pretty godawful breath and a beard too! I opened my eyes and saw a scruffy dog — beady black eyes and a cool, moist nostril an inch away from my face. He disappeared back into the woods by the time I sat up. But I swear I had more energy and strength than ever before."

"You came face to face with the Divine." The words just tumbled out without Solomon really thinking them through.

Leclair raised an eyebrow and gave the priest a good, long, incredulous glare.

"I'm talking about a fuckin' dog, *Father*. Are you going all goofball on me?"

Solomon nodded his head in a way that indicated he both acknowledged and didn't that Leclair had a valid point. "I think what I am saying, perhaps not very well, is that you entered the Kingdom of God, in a sense, simply by recognizing the face of the Creator in creation. In some small and maybe inexplicable way, every creature on earth reveals to you His many faces. You know, even in a life filled mostly with doubt, I can't seem to expel Saint Patrick's words from my head. It's where he speaks about Christ being within us, behind us, before us, beside us, beneath us and above us — here, everywhere to comfort us. The only way I can make any sense of that is by seeing a sliver of the Divine in every creature."

"Right." Leclair's response hovered somewhere between dismissive and reflective. "Well, I'm not sure what's hocus-pocus and what's not."

"It was *you* who came to see *me*, not the other way around. Look, this is the kingdom, right here. It's being built here and now, every day and by everyone. That's not some Houdini trick, Joseph."

Leclair nodded, somewhat dismissively. His voice had become barely audible. "Well, I'm not doing much building…"

Solomon felt completely drained; he couldn't manage any more comforting. He was convinced that he could no longer muster the energy to string together another sentence. So without getting up and without speaking, he cleared his throat, pointed to the knife and stretched out his good hand, palm up. Leclair hesitated and spent what felt like an eternity staring at the knife before extracting it from the bark of the tree, walking over to Solomon and dropping it into the snow.

Leclair faced away. "You can go now..."

Solomon looked confused, though Leclair didn't turn around to see it.

"Here, take these too..." Without facing Solomon, he tossed a set of keys towards the priest.

"What are you doing?" Solomon sounded exasperated. He was so worn out that he felt on the verge of tears.

"You said this is the kingdom. So why don't you let me enjoy it in peace..." Bitterness and defeat coloured Leclair's voice.

Solomon did not move.

"Look, I appreciate you coming out here and all, and thanks for last night at the motel. But get lost, eh?"

"You seriously expect me to just leave you out here?" Solomon was incredulous.

Leclair walked up close to the priest with a threatening air. Solomon still sat in the same spot, looking pathetic and small.

"What other choice do you have?" He paused, before making the sign of the cross in front of Solomon.

"There. I've absolved you, Father. Now go. There's a quarter tank of gas left in the truck."

**

Holding the steering wheel with one hand proved more cumbersome than Solomon thought it would. But he coped. When he got back to the rectory that afternoon, he decided against lying down on his bed, even though during the seemingly endless drive, his ascetic little room beckoned like some lush oasis. No, he couldn't lie down. The mop and bucket next to the confessional lured him into the type of mundane work that promised to dull his senses — like some taboo drug. He just didn't care. Or more properly put, he just couldn't *afford* to care. More properly still, he aspired to indifference.

The light filtering through the stained glass cast circular and octagonal pools of green, yellow, blue and purple on the stone floor. Solomon caught himself rubbing the mop with absent-minded vigour, trying in vain to erase the coloured light, before he realized what he was doing. He felt silly. Enough of this. As he lifted the bucket of grey water and poured it into the toilet, careful not to splash the sides, he didn't hear the high-pitched ring of the phone in his bedroom puncture the stale air and the silence. In its persistence, the pulsating ring, now somehow smoother and less urgent than before, travelled through the walls, out the fogged-up windows, and swirled around the steeple. It ascended nimbly towards a sea of milky clouds that craved nothing more than to finally part before the presence of that dilly-dallier of a spring.

David and Franco

David *really* didn't want to be seen like this. Bathing naked in the Ottawa River — shampoo in his hair and a scrawny lily-white body glistening in the morning sun — was not a good look for him. And despite the self-satisfying pretense that society here was a liberal, open-minded and inclusive beacon for the world, David had the book knowledge to understand that by European standards, people were more prudish than they cared to admit, particularly when it came to nude bodies.

David rubbed his socks against a bar of soap, mindful not to let his underwear float away or sink to the murky bottom of the river. He worried that if he didn't hurry up, one of the colourless, profoundly law-abiding civil servants on their way to work would scold him for mistaking the Outaouais for the Ganges. David didn't feel purified, but at least the grubbiness of a humid night, where his clammy skin touched the canvas of his tent, had been washed away.

There was something almost fraudulent about David's makeshift campsite and his river bath. In his mind, he saw himself as Chris from *Into the Wild*, courageously fleeing urban civilization and the comforts of modernity to live a simple life, retreating ever further into the wilderness. The problem was that David's home in the wild was an illusion. Not too far away and well within his line of vision, grey concrete high-rises from the 1970s towered uncomfortably in the hot, hazy air. The narrow beach and clearing that served as his home was separated from the busy Macdonald Parkway by a strip of forest little wider than a suburban backyard. Barely a hundred metres to the north lay a public beach, complete with a bar that tried too hard to seem exotic and with wannabe hippies who showed up at night in groups — guitars, dreadlocks and pot.

The little battery-operated radio sitting outside David's tent was a veritable beast in disguise. The sound quality may have been tinny, but it was loud enough to drown out the morning rush-hour traffic on the parkway.

"Do you have an *embarrassing* and uncomfortable fungal infection in one or more of your toenails? Are your toenails discoloured, deformed or crumbling away at the tip? Is *shame* forcing you to cover up, when you'd like nothing more than to wear sandals or flip-flops? Thanks to groundbreaking technology developed by Moor & Shum International, we can give your toenails a new lease on life. Call us for a hassle-free consultation with Dr. Vera Moor or Head Nurse Emmet Shum. We'll get your toes *back on track*!"

David inspected his toes with some satisfaction before laying his freshly rinsed socks out on a rock to dry. He hunted for an extra pair in his backpack. The clinic's toll-free number was pre-empted a little too early by the morning show's host. On air, Bob came across as your typical middle-class suburban Canadian dad: folksy, moderately conservative, charmingly uncomplicated and probably a master at barbecues.

"It's gonna be a real scorcher again today, folks! Thirty degrees, thirty-eight with the humidex and you're listening to CCRB 600, family-friendly talk radio for the nation's capital. Telling it like it is. The hard-working, Canadian taxpayer's source for no-nonsense analysis on what's going on in this, well, pretty messed-up world of ours. And to help sort things out for you, here's our very own frank-talking Franco Ritchie. So, what do you have for us today?"

"And a good morning to all of you, and to you as well, Bob! Well, let me tell you, I think we all need to give thanks to the good Lord today that we don't live in Greece — and it's not just about their crumbling old buildings. Have you been there, Bob? I mean they're really *crumbling*."

"Greece? Nah. We do Florida with the kids. We don't give our money to the *commies*." Bob's congenial tone turned briefly to indignation.

"Right on, Bob, right on! The Greeks have fifty percent unemployment among the youth and now they wanna suck the western taxpayers dry to bail 'em out!"

David stopped puttering about his campsite and sat down on a rock across from the radio. Somehow Franco Ritchie demanded his full attention. He sounded oddly foreign to David. Franco Ritchie had an exaggerated southern drawl, which was not entirely convincing, mixed with big-talking self-confidence reminiscent of a used car salesman or a low-rent, shady lawyer hunting for clients.

"But don't you go thinking that it's not all coming here, that it won't be impacting you, spreading like a virus! We're all going to feel the creeping danger of rising unemployment, of poverty, on our own skins, of deciding whether you can afford that doughnut and coffee at Timmies today or if you'll need to bring your Folgers Instant in a thermos from home. It's coming folks, you just wait and see! It's like terrorism ... or the plague. People didn't believe it till it was dangling over us on that red horizon!"

David felt that tossing and turning in the pit of his stomach that comes with rising anxiety. Or was it hunger? He was glued to the radio and hoped beyond hope that

Franco's story would end well. He craved reassurance from this domineering, faceless voice.

"People! We need to be alert and we need to be vigilant. From now on, *each and every one of us* has to look over our shoulders every time we turn the corner!" Franco's voice rose to a fever pitch and David began to feel nauseated.

"*Jesus Christ*, Frankie ... that's enough to put the fear of God into all of us." Bob sounded despondent and alarmed. He almost whispered, as if privy to a horrific secret conspiracy.

"Look, Bob, the good news is that you're not alone." For the first time, Franco sounded soothing, believable and Canadian. Gone was the southern drawl. "I know that many of you are already feeling the pinch of the collections agencies hounding you. Oh, I see you opening up the mail every morning fearing that *today* is when that eviction notice will finally arrive. But if we stand together, we can solve this. We can *fight* this!"

The queasy feeling in David's stomach began to subside. The tightness in his chest dissipated. But the hunger became more pronounced. He retrieved a hard-boiled egg from the bottom of his backpack and smelled it. It seemed fine.

"Look, I'm not here to boast, but I've helped scores of talented young men and women climb back from the brink. I teach 'em to turn their backs on a lifetime of failure. I've brought hope to dozens, no — to hundreds! God only knows, I don't do it for the money or the fame. In fact, just so you know that I put my money where my mouth is, I have an incredible offer for all my loyal listeners and followers out there. If you get to my office today no later than noon, you can experience what Franco Ritchie's life-coaching can do for you, for just nineteen ninety-nine. I mean, *wow*! Buy and control your future for mere pocket change!"

David turned off his radio suddenly and looked at the time on his cellphone. It was 8:45 AM. Unopened letters, mostly unpaid bills, stuck out from his backpack. He stuffed them back in, along with the only two books he brought with him: Margaret Laurence's *The Diviners* and an anthology of poetry from Philip Larkin. He smiled and started pacing with a growing degree of enthusiasm. He felt that he was realistic in his expectations. He wasn't looking for a get-rich-quick scheme nor did he ever aspire to be a millionaire. He wasn't sure if it was a lack of cutthroat ambition, but he didn't think this was down to laziness. All he knew for sure was that he had to make a success of his move to the city. That meant finding employment, making enough money to rent his own apartment and pay his way, and maybe send home a hundred dollars each month to help his chronically depressed father and his overworked, increasingly desperate mother with their groceries.

David didn't have a mirror, but based on the dark reflection in his cellphone screen, almost too hot to touch from sitting out in the sun, he looked all right. His white dress shirt seemed as though it had been freshly ironed, his pants were perfectly pleated and his tie was just right: conservative, but not dowdy. He looked like the quintessential Mormon missionary. If only he would stop losing weight. He used his pocket knife to poke a new hole through his belt. That solved that problem. But there was nothing he could do about the growing, gaping chasm between his throat and his now oversized collar shirt.

As he walked into the city, the foolishness of not wearing an undershirt dawned on him. The back of his shirt was soaked as he trudged through the merciless humidity. There seemed to be no respite from the scorching sun either. By the time he found himself amidst the eclectic mix of commercial establishments and dreary low-rise office buildings of Bank Street, he was sweating profusely. Admittedly, he also felt a little nervous about his encounter with the man on the radio, who this morning first took him to the depths of anguish and impending global ruin before lighting the pathway to redemption.

**

David couldn't figure out how on earth Franco Ritchie managed to stuff such a large piece of sushi into his mouth all at once. His cheeks seemed about to burst, but he managed to shift the sushi around in his mouth and he calmly chewed and swallowed like a pro, all while David sat across his desk, not knowing if it was impolite to stare. He looked away at the stained and faded Santa coffee mug on the window ledge.

"Okay, go! I'm listening." Franco didn't make eye contact as he gingerly dipped sushi into a small container of soy sauce and smelled it, looking slightly concerned, before stuffing it in his mouth.

David felt as though the starting pistol had just gone off in a marathon and he was expected to bolt. He couldn't gather his thoughts and wasn't sure what Franco wanted to know.

"Well, I'm kinda new here. I just arrived a couple of days ago … and I heard you on the radio, so I, um, I thought that maybe I should see you?" David stopped awkwardly.

Franco took a gulp from a slime-green energy drink. It was disconcerting to David that he couldn't really see Franco's eyes through those tinted glasses. It wasn't particularly bright in that office, but the glasses on Franco's face had gone dark nonetheless.

"You can stop right there, David. I know everything there is to know about you, just by looking at you … just by looking into your eyes…" David was visibly taken aback.

"Oh, that's right, David! That small-town, farm-boy mentality … the deer-in-the-headlights stare as you realize that you're lost here in the big city. You're *lost* in this jungle of towering glass and steel! You're weak and you're insignificant! You're just a little speck of dust bouncing around in this big bad world, aren't you now, David?" Franco leaned back in his chair and put his feet on the desk with a self-satisfied grin as he let that diagnosis sink in.

"Well, I'm not sure that I really think that of myself…" David was uncertain. Should he be agreeing with Franco?

Suddenly Franco's tone changed and he sat up.

"David, *David*! You're dripping all over my office. Poor kid, you must be nervous and scared. Here, wipe yourself up." Franco tossed a box of tissues right into David's lap before turning on a desk fan and sitting it directly across from his client. It blew a combination of hot air and dust right into David's face.

"How long you been out of work?"

"I just graduated a few months ago…"

"In what?" Franco sounded as though he was about to pounce and David was well aware of this.

"I have a BA honours degree in Canadian literature."

"Canadian lit, eh?" Franco scoffed. "That's like — what — *Anne of Green Gables*?" Franco gulped down more of his energy drink.

David felt profoundly insulted, and his sentence came out as though he was sulking. "There's more to it than that…"

"Yeah? And what's it done for you so far, David? Look it, I'm here to help you rise out of the gutter, to scrape you up from the streets and move you into the fast-paced world of finance, Armani suits, silk ties, lunches at the Château Laurier, champagne dinners." He stopped mid-sentence and leaned in close to David. "*Six figures!*"

David wasn't sure how to respond.

"Oh, okay. I never really thought about that…"

"Of course you didn't. Do you have family?"

"No, not really…" David didn't feel it would help to disclose his parents' unhappiness and their pitiful state. But Franco drilled on.

"Mother? Father? Money? Estates?"

David cast his eyes down and Franco seemed to know not to press further.

"Okay, look, don't worry about it." Franco displayed what seemed to be a glimmer of compassion, as though he realized that he had touched on something sensitive.

Franco looked down to the wall-to-wall carpeting and noticed the dirt that David had tracked in.

"Holy shit! Where the hell have you been?"

At first David was confused, but once he looked behind him, he could see what Franco was talking about.

"Oh, jeez. Sorry about that, I didn't—"

"Would you do that to your potential future employer? Great start, great first impression. All right. Get up, *get up!*" David stood up reluctantly, not knowing what was coming next.

"Now get out of my office!" Franco roared and then started typing feverishly on his keyboard.

"What?" David couldn't believe his ears. This was it?

"Out!" Franco pointed to the door before returning to his furious typing. David looked down for a moment and it wasn't clear to him if Franco was actually typing coherent words and sentences or simply giving his computer a good beating.

But he knew that he didn't have time to ponder that. He walked to the door, deflated and dejected. His body language said it all. Just as he opened the door, Franco barked out another order.

"All right, get back in here. I've made an exception. I'm going to forgive you. Now how does that sound, David?"

David was stunned and had no clue what to say.

"You're welcome. Now leave your shoes at the door and sit back down."

David did as he was told. He felt like he was in the middle of a dizzying whirlwind and was unable to get his bearings. Was it Franco or the fact that he was hungry?

"What do you believe, David?"

"What do you mean?"

"I mean what do you believe deep down inside, Davey? Everyone's gotta believe in something. I can't help you if you have no faith." Franco opened his desk drawer and pulled out a tray holding a wide range of religious symbols and items. He poured it all out onto his desk. From the pile of prayer beads, rosaries, Stars of David and tiny plastic Virgin Marys, he shook out a kippah and put it on his head, slightly crooked. He slowly dangled a rosary in front of David, like a pendulum, and lifted his eyebrows. "So? What is it?"

David smiled. "Looks like you're well equipped!"

Franco kept dangling the rosary, staring at David, waiting for his response. He wasn't going to let him off the hook. On some level, David wondered if Franco was pulling his leg.

"So where do you keep the Kool-Aid?" David's grin widened, but Franco at first seemed perplexed before frowning disapprovingly.

"It's just a cultural reference to something that happened once … in a jungle." Franco kept staring, growing increasingly irritated. "But it's not really important, just—"

"Look, don't play those artsy games with me! I'm not into that shit. If I'm gonna help you, you need to be an open book when you're with me. You like books, don't you? All you have to do is open the gates and let me in." Franco reached across the desk and poked David's chest multiple times, as he was speaking. "Let me help you help yourself, Davey."

"Well, that's why I'm here…"

"Good. You'll need to start attending a church or a synagogue. Take your pick. They're some of the best venues for networking. You know, getting your name out there. Maybe consider joining the Freemasons too. You'd be surprised how many connections you'll make. I'd tell you to consider joining a mosque, it's just that I don't have any experience with the Muslims yet. But I'm working on it, Davey, you better believe it! I'm very open-minded that way."

Franco didn't seem to require a response or verbal commitment, and David found that reassuring. Instead, Franco appeared busy fumbling with a stack of papers in a drawer.

"Right then. You're gonna have to give all your information to my secretary: date of birth, SIN number, phone, home address. I need to know everything. Are you a criminal?"

David was stunned and offended.

"No!"

"Gotta ask. Just wait a minute while I call her…" Franco started tapping his fingers on the desk as he waited for the secretary to answer.

"Shit, she's on her lunch break already … typical. I'll have a little chat with her when she gets back. Here, fill this out until then." Franco handed David a clipboard with a form. He was taken aback by one of the first questions.

"Why do you need to know my waist size?"

"Because, Davey my friend, I am going to shop you around with some of the movers and shakers in town. And that cheap shit you're wearing now isn't gonna cut it. I won't have you dressed like some office monkey or a cheapskate accountant. This is the real deal, Shakespeare. I don't bullshit.

I'm setting you up with an amazing opening. If you get this one, you'll never look back. But get ready: things are going to speed up from here on in."

***

Located in a Victorian red-brick house just off Somerset, Moor and Shum International turned out to be much fancier than David thought it would be. It felt more like a luxurious spa than a clinic. The soothing sound of water trickling over rocks and a hint of eucalyptus filled the parlour where two women in matching plush purple bathrobes sat next to each other with their feet soaking in bronze tubs. A man wearing a lime-green robe lay on a settee with a hot towel covering his entire face, except for the tip of his nose.

David stood in the middle of the parlour, feeling out of place, until a man in blue scrubs, who was around his age, peeked out from the door at the far end.

"That guy's here!"

David swore the man in scrubs rolled his eyes and sounded irritated. A thin, small woman with severely straight short hair, a perma-tan and several gold bracelets dangling like little chimes on her wrist, appeared. She gave what David took to be a scolding look to the man in scrubs before smiling at David and walking towards him confidently, right hand extended.

"You must be David. Franco has said nothing but great things about you. It's a pleasure…"

"Hi. Are you Dr. Vera Moor?"

"The one and only!" She smiled and introduced her assistant. "And you've met Head Nurse Shum?"

Head Nurse Shum sighed, as he glanced up at the grand chandelier in the parlour.

"Pleasure to meet you, Head Nurse Shum." David smiled innocuously at the man who failed to soften his demeanour.

"Likewise." Shum's voice sounded as though it had been flattened by a freight train.

It bothered David that Shum clearly didn't like him one bit. He wasn't aware of anyone ever hating him before. Having someone audibly scoff and visibly dismiss him *before* a job interview wasn't reassuring. It seemed like a particularly bad time to start being despised.

They walked into Dr. Vera's office. The doctor took her seat behind the mahogany desk, while Shum sat at her side. The wall behind her was covered in a sea of diplomas, though too high up to read. Her desk was lined with thank-you cards from satisfied patients. One of the cards was turned David's way, so he could see the inscription:

Dear Dr. Vera:

I can never thank you enough for giving back my husband's self-confidence. You can't even begin to imagine the joy he brings me — it's like day and night. We have finally consummated our marriage. We are expecting our little Álvaro in October.

"David, we have more success stories than we can count. I have to say that we are very protective of our institution, aren't we, Head Nurse Shum?" The man in the scrubs crossed his legs, leaned back in his chair and glared at David. "We require *just* the right person to work our door and greet our patients. It takes the perfect mix of compassion and plain old business smarts to treat them with dignity while making sure they understand their horrible predicament. Does that make sense to you, David?"

"Yes, completely! My dad ran a small business and he always seemed to build a great relationship with his customers."

Shum sighed audibly.

"There are no *customers* here. Just patients."

"Emmet, *please*. David is just giving a personal example. That's what candidates do in competitive interviews..." Dr. Vera turned to David and smiled. "Now as you can see, Head Nurse Shum and I care about our institution deeply. To be entirely honest with you, we have a strong preference for an attractive young woman to fill the role for which you applied. Our female patients are more comfortable when greeted by a woman and our male patients are generally uneasy when they see a man working behind a receptionist's desk. But despite all this, I have a deep respect for Franco and his gorgeous wife, Lina, so we are here to give you a chance. Sound fair?"

David forced a smile and thanked Dr. Vera for considering him for the job.

"Good! Head Nurse Shum, why don't you open with the first question..."

The man in scrubs leaned even further back in his chair, tilted his head and examined David with an air of incredulity.

"So, what's a BA good for anyway?"

David couldn't conceal his dismay and surprise.

"What's a BA good for? I mean, I like to think that it teaches you to analyze difficult, complex texts, to read between the lines, to communicate effectively both in writing and verbally. To appreciate nuance. And to have an inquisitive mind." In the pause, David was initially pleased with his answer, but then seemed glum, as he realized just by looking at them that he must have said something wrong.

Dr. Vera cleared her throat and interlaced her fingers.

"How's your French, David? We do get the odd French patient and we like to share the good news with them in their mother tongue."

David felt nervous but took a deep breath. He knew exactly what he had to do.

"Oui, je parle français aussi. À l'école, je prenais des cours de français pendant cinq ans. Comme un adolescent, je lisais Voltaire et Diderot pendant le week-end. Juste pour le fun!" David closed with a big smile, which faded rapidly.

"We've got a real keener," Head Nurse Shum noted bitterly. "Can you do Mandarin now?"

"Emmet!" Dr. Vera looked disapprovingly at her assistant, who seemed nonetheless satisfied with himself. "Well, as I said before, we are very protective of what we have built. Now tell me, David — can you send us a copy of your credit history?"

"Oh, you need my personal credit history? Yeah, I guess I could get you a copy..."

"Excellent. And how about four professional references? We'll need them by tomorrow, please."

David felt all hope drain away.

"Four? I'm really eager to grow with your company, but I just graduated from university, so I only have a little experience. But I'm looking forward to learning from you and I'm great when given training and direction." David smiled, but was not sure if he had convinced them. Shum scowled, but he thought Dr. Vera looked sympathetic.

"Good personal hygiene and appearance are very important in instilling confidence, David. Our patients expect it of us. We can provide you with the right clothing and we have instructions for you to take to your barber, should we decide to offer you this job. But tell me, David, how are your teeth?"

"Uh, I think they're fine..."

"Yes, well, we'll have to get Head Nurse Shum to give them a quick inspection."

Before David could protest, Shum rolled his stool directly in front of David, grabbed and pulled down his jaw with one hand and lifted his upper lips with the other — a veritable invasion.

Shum turned to Dr. Vera and shook his head disapprovingly.

"David, I believe what Head Nurse Shum means is that if we were to hire you, we would have to get your teeth bleached. It is so important to be able to smile confidently when discussing treatment options and payment plans with our patients."

David had not yet gotten over the shock of Shum's surprise inspection when Dr. Vera continued.

"I do have one very important question for you, David. It's a scenario, and I'd like to see how you would respond. Let's say a new patient is struggling with a bad case of toenail fungus, recently diagnosed and confirmed by Head Nurse Shum. We send her to the receptionist's desk with two treatment plan options. Option A is a basic, generic solution that includes a commitment to five treatments only. Option B is a commitment to a full-year plan, with two treatments per month, a box of self-help DVDs, an inspirational calendar and a special mug as a gift. Which would you encourage our patient to purchase?"

David's self-confidence returned to him and he sat up straight in his chair.

"I would make sure to get a feel for what our patient can afford and if I sensed that she had the disposable income for Option B, I would try to share with her the benefits of this plan. You see, I believe firmly in fair play. I know that you need to make a profit, and I think it's possible to do that without exploiting anyone. I'm a strong believer in that. Unwavering, actually!"

***

Franco sat in silent disbelief. Then: "You didn't say that. You didn't fuckin' say that! Holy shit, David!"

"What? It wasn't *that* bad, was it?" David felt thoroughly confused. He was convinced that he had given a thoughtful response. And he felt much better at the end of the interview, when he noticed that Shum finally smiled pleasantly as he sent him on his way.

"No, not bad at all from a village idiot who hasn't managed to wash off the manure from his boots!" Franco tossed his phone in front of him on the desk. David felt genuinely hurt.

"That's not called for. Look, I didn't come here to get abused…"

"Oh, so now you're a sissy too? Jesus, it's like you climbed out of some cave … which reminds me, the address you gave me doesn't add up. Your postal code's wrong. I need you to give me the correct one, and ASAP!"

David sulked quietly for a moment.

"Look, I'm just tired. I need to go home."

Franco raised his eyebrows and fell back in his chair.

"Really? Tired? You're telling *me* that *you're* tired? I'm in this office sixteen hours a day, including on fucking Sundays. I sleep with my phone on my chest so that if there's a deal at three in the morning, I'll feel the vibration and I'll be ready to jump on it!"

"I guess that's just not me," said David, in resignation.

"No shit, it's not you. You prefer jerking off with Shakespeare, taking your sweet old time with things and being all Mary Poppins in interviews!"

David looked deeply resentful as he glared at Franco.

"Look, fine … I get it. Your first interview wasn't stellar. Maybe we'll try again tomorrow, but we won't reach for the stars just yet, okay?" David refused to respond. He looked like an insulted child.

"Did you hear me?"

***

David sat on the bench at the abandoned bus stop, lost in thought. He felt compelled to call home, even though chatting with his mother was taxing at the best of times. And it was definitely not the best of times. Ever since his father lost the business two years ago and suffered a nervous breakdown, his mother was left to pick up the pieces. At first, she took it in stride and almost relished the challenge. While Dad stared listlessly at his tools in the basement and came up only when he was called to eat dinner or to sleep, his mother methodically sold off what she could to make ends meet. First went the spare television. Then the main one too. She packed up her mother-in-law's china and shipped it to the auction house. David came home one day and found the oil painting in the living room was gone — only the nail and a discoloured rectangular space on the wall marked where it had once been.

Every time he arrived home from university, the house looked emptier and Dad retreated further into the basement. Eventually, his mother succumbed to perpetual bitterness and to the liquor cabinet that beckoned in the corner of the dining room — she never sold that off. David worked part-time hours at the hardware store one town over to help out, but there was no bus to take him home at night. He got accustomed to walking the eight kilometres along the old highway. It was awful in the winter, but other than that, at least it gave him an opportunity to think and clear his head.

He dialled home on his cellphone, but rather than ringing, an automated message greeted him.

"We're sorry, outgoing calls are not possible at this time. Please remain on the line as we connect you to our Accounts Receivable department. Please have your account information ready."

"Not again…" David rubbed his eyes and tossed his phone into his backpack. He searched for something to eat and found half a chocolate bar. He devoured it, and it seemed as though nothing had ever tasted so good.

He was less queasy and that bench was now tempting him relentlessly to lie down. It was an *abandoned* bus stop after all. Based on the tattered sign, the bus route had been suspended for a while now. The chance of anyone walking by and seeing him was slim. But he wasn't sure he could ever get himself to do it — sleeping in public, on a bench, was a psychological threshold he couldn't seem to allow himself to cross. His vulnerability was on full display for the world to see. It was the ultimate defeat. And once he gave up that last shred of dignity, could he ever really get it back?

***

The phone kept ringing in Franco's office, but Franco just glared at it and refused to answer. David was getting annoyed.

"You can pick that up, you know. I can wait."

"Never you mind, Shakespeare. My secretary will deal with it."

"Oh, will I meet her today?"

Franco glanced at David suspiciously.

"We'll see. Hopefully she'll be in on time today. She's such a mess, that woman. But I feel for her. I'm giving her a second chance and all. Kinda like I gave you a second chance too, David."

"Well, maybe she's the one who tried to call you. Maybe she's stuck in traffic … or something like that."

"Okay, Shakespeare. Let's get your life in order first. How does that sound?" Franco sneered. "I have a new opportunity lined up for you today. I think it will be good for you. You won't be getting onto your private jet just yet, but let me tell you from experience, sometimes you gotta start off at the bottom. If you're bright, you'll make it to the top in no time. Trust me, that's how it works around here."

"I'll give it a shot. What do you have in mind?"

The phone rang again. Franco looked at it with deepening irritation.

"Go ahead, really. Do you want me to leave while you take that?"

Franco thought about it briefly. "I'll just be a moment. Go wait outside in the corridor."

David leaned against the grey wall in a deserted, sterile-looking hallway. He heard snippets faintly through the door, especially when Franco raised his voice.

"As I've already told you, I sent it in two days ago … yes, it was through bank transfer … RBC, like usual. What do you mean, what was the reason? I was busy. Are you gonna hang me for it? … Yes, yes, yes. I'll need until the end of the month though."

David felt weak and faint as he stood against the wall. He probably looked unwell too. He slid down against the wall until he hit the floor. It felt good to sit, but as soon as he hit the carpet, Franco swung open the door and motioned for him to come back in.

David sat quietly in the chair, pale and listless.

"Franco..."

"What?" Franco stared intensely at his computer screen.

"Would you mind if I took one?" David spoke sheepishly as he pointed to a basket of what appeared to be Halloween chocolates.

Franco looked perplexed.

"Go ahead. I don't care."

"Thanks. It's just that I haven't had breakfast. I'm feeling a bit light-headed..." David unwrapped a ball of chocolate-covered peanut butter.

"Well, I tough it out without breakfast most mornings. An espresso is all I need, Shakespeare."

"I wasn't able to eat supper last night either..."

Franco peered through the top of his tinted glasses.

"What, you were *that* upset? Or you're on a diet or something?"

"Sort of." David looked down, visibly embarrassed, as he unwrapped a second chocolate.

Franco squinted at him in silence and then grabbed an apple from the window ledge behind him and tossed it into David's lap.

"Here. An apple a day. You know the rest."

"Oh! Thanks, Franco. You sure?"

"Listen, let's get back to business. I've got an opportunity for you. Keep an open mind. You're starting small, but I'll build you up. Just be flexible and don't fuck up this time!"

***

"So how ya doin' Dave?" Bob had congeniality down to an art. The interview was set in front of a doughnut shop. By the time David arrived, a tall man in his forties, dressed in a T-shirt, a baseball cap, shorts and flip-flops stood there with two coffees. Bob used his newly leased car as his office. It proved both economical and practical, since he was always on the go. He would happily use a meeting room down at the radio station, but times were tough and the station manager started charging freelancers if they wanted to book space for personal use. David felt awkward but made sure to congratulate Bob on his new vehicle. He then reassured him that he would do the same: "Why waste good money on meeting spaces?" He pushed some dog toys away with his shoes.

"Oh, the missus loves it too! Maybe next time I'll let you take it for a spin, bud. It's a beast!"

David smiled and said how much he would look forward to that. This wasn't the time to disclose that he didn't have a licence.

"Okay, now buddy, I'm not sure how much Franco told you about my project, but here's the deal. It looks like I perfected the cure for male pattern baldness." Bob took off his baseball cap to reveal an almost entirely bald head, except for what looked like patchy orange peach fuzz on the top. "Six months ago, I was smooth as a hard-boiled egg. But look at me now, eh?"

"Oh, yes, I see something growing…"

"Do you ever!" Bob put his cap back on. "Now look it, you're a good kid, but you do seem a little overqualified for this kinda sales work, eh."

"I'm overqualified?" David couldn't hide his alarm. "So should I have left that degree off of my resumé?"

Bob waved his hand dismissively.

"No, no. Not at all. It's just that I'm not sure you'd be all that happy in this line of work, bud. You're a real smart kid, you know. But I got no problem having you give it a shot. Here, just smell this." Bob handed David a large bottle of his homemade, revolutionary lotion. David popped open the cap and the whiff of garlic mixed with what smelled like mothballs hit him hard.

"Oh, wow. Ah, I think that I can *totally* get excited about your hair growth lotion." He tried to marshal more enthusiasm. "You know, I can just imagine what a difference this lotion would have made in my father's life. He really struggled with his receding hairline. He would have just loved this! Come to think of it, my mother would have loved it too!" David smiled awkwardly.

"I'm loving your enthusiasm, Dave. But don't worry — I won't have you doing sales right away. How about we get your feet wet with a little data entry first. You can help with the invoices, the mailing and the customer relations. I'll get the missus to set you up with a nice little work station in my basement."

David couldn't believe it. He was genuinely thrilled and could barely contain himself in Bob's stuffy car. He wanted to jump out and start running through the parking lot.

"Absolutely! I've always had a real passion for data entry. I'm a fantastic organizer. Back when I was living at home, I always kept my room in order, even as a child. I used to take out all the Lego from the box, divide it by colour and then line it up according to size! Dad thought I was crazy and Mom thought I had the type of OCD that you could outgrow. Oh sir, you should have seen me. I used to do that with my mom's knives too, organizing them according to size and different types of edges. Whenever I could, I'd be sure to polish them too! I guess you can say I am still sort of OCD, eh?" David laughed with a mix of eagerness and excitement.

***

Franco massaged his temple.

"I kind of thought I did well this time..."

"Yeah ... if I had sent you out to audition for a role in *American Psycho*, you would have done just great, Shakespeare."

David noticed the stack of unopened mail on Franco's desk. One envelope read "Important Invoice Enclosed."

"Well, I guess if you ever needed a secretary to open your mail, you'd think of me?" David spoke sheepishly, but Franco didn't seem amused.

"Franco, I don't know how to say this, but I'm getting pretty desperate for something. *Anything*."

Franco looked glum. He had no response.

"Just based on your radio announcement, I really thought that you could help me. You seem to be so well connected and you're confident." David's voice trailed off until it sounded like he was mostly speaking to himself. "Maybe too confident…"

Defensiveness awoke Franco from whatever mental rut he had been in.

"Of course I'm gonna help! Look, Davey. The summer's a bad time to find employment in any city. But you came to me for a reason! You woke up that morning to my voice and something that I said struck you, deep down inside that simple, honest farm-boy heart of yours." Franco paused and smiled. "You know what? I've got it! Yes, I've got it!" He slammed his desk. David looked interested.

"I know this really lovely older — no, sorry — *mature* woman who needs some help around the house. I sometimes send guys like you, down on their luck, over to her. At least you'll make a few bucks while we set you up with something permanent. Dame Wanda…" Franco coughed and looked away. "She's a real treasure, just a lovely woman!"

"Okay…" David paused with uncertainty in his voice. "What will I have to do?"

Franco let out a brief cough again. "Oh, just some basic tasks: mowing her lawn, pulling out her weeds, maybe doing some groceries for her. It's not rocket science, believe me," he laughed. "But it will put some change into your pockets. And from the looks of it, you could use a bit of cash…"

***

Dame Wanda seemed well pleased as David stood uncertainly on her porch.

"Oh, this is splendid, *just splendid.*" She beamed as she looked up and down at David and clutched her pearl necklace absent-mindedly. "I say, that old kipper got it right at last!"

The portly woman's abdomen seemed ready to flee her body through her tight orange-and-pink polyester gown.

David smiled awkwardly. He felt like the shy schoolboy adults find excessively cute and feel compelled to pinch on the cheek or pat on the head.

"Dame Wanda? Franco sent me to help you with your garden…"

The smile vanished from Dame Wanda's face. She suddenly appeared taken aback and her hands travelled from her pearl necklace to her hips.

"Garden? Now what's this I hear about a garden?"

David stared at her pathetically.

"Oh, this is *most* inopportune…" Dame Wanda seemed momentarily lost in her thoughts, before returning to being irritated. "Very well, enter, *enter*! Conversing on the porch like this is rather too common, I am afraid. You shall have some Jaffa cakes and cream and *I* shall get to the bottom of this terrible misunderstanding!"

Dame Wanda's home smelled of frankincense. David felt increasingly alarmed when he noticed that the curtains in the living room were pulled and candles were lit in all corners, providing a certain ambience. A fuchsia statue of Buddha occupied the centre of the coffee table, in front of which sat a basket of overly ripe fruit, burning incense and votives. In every corner of the home sat a knick-knack or collectible, and the walls resembled those of an overstocked commercial art gallery. The space, though large, felt claustrophobic.

"I shall thank you to mind the Rhodesian copper tray on the end table!" Dame Wanda didn't even glance over at David, who sat in the far side of the living room near the corner of the couch, as she dialled from a darkened alcove. "My late husband brought it back from Salisbury. I am sure you will have noticed that nearly every nation or territory is represented here. I like to say that the sun never sets on this house." Dame Wanda cleared her throat and resumed her pearl clutching.

"Ritchie? Dame Wanda! I say, I face a most unpleasant predicament once again as a result of your fiendish machinations! Does it pain you to speak honestly with the young gentlemen in your employ? You know very well that it is not my garden that requires tending. I dare say, we have been through this before, Ritchie!"

Dame Wanda glanced over at David, who helped himself to another Jaffa cake from a crystal bowl on the coffee table. He usually wasn't hungry when he was this nervous, but he had to eat something. He felt light-headed again.

"You say that he is amenable to addressing my needs, do you? Very well, we shall see. But you understand, Ritchie, that this leaves me in a most delicate position." Dame Wanda put down the phone without a good-bye, walked over to David and sat across from him in the oversized burgundy wing chair. He slowly stuffed the last of the Jaffa cake into his mouth and realized that he wouldn't be able to respond until he swallowed.

"I should make it perfectly clear to you, young man, that what I ask of you is strictly therapeutic in nature. I shall not tolerate any unconscionable conduct whilst you are tending to my needs, and I say this with particular respect to those moments when I might be in a more vulnerable position. May I assume that this is understood, yes?"

David worried that the sticky, chewed-up ball of pastry would get stuck in his throat. He swallowed hard and felt it slide down slowly, then nodded his head slightly in uncertain agreement. Dame Wanda's facial muscles eased.

"I am told that you are a master of high diction..." David raised an eyebrow. "As I am sure you can appreciate, I shall expect nothing less than high diction whilst you are providing me with my therapy."

***

Franco seemed immensely satisfied as he slid some toonies and loonies across the desk to David, who looked dishevelled and held his head in his hands.

"You did good, Davey. Don't worry about it one bit! Dame Wanda called me right after you left. She gave you a rave review. Good job!"

"That's why she only paid eleven bucks?" David sounded so disappointed that he seemed ready to cry.

Franco cleared his throat.

"Well no, no. Not quite. I had to take my cut. I'm very modest with that sort of thing. A percentage here, a percentage there — a nice office like this doesn't just grow on trees, you know. Cheer up, Davey! Buy yourself a cheeseburger. You're losing weight. We need to keep you able-bodied!"

***

Back home, the campfire roared and crackled as David gulped down his second can of beer. He crumpled it up and hurled it at a tree but missed by a good two feet. He never had much of a throw. David picked up the anthology of Philip Larkin poems. It was lying in the dirt near the fire. He opened it to "Aubade" and hunched over to read the text in the growing darkness.

Every now and then, the neon lights of a bus cut through the trees as it sped into the night along Macdonald Parkway. One by one, the lit windows of the grey high-rises that crowded on the distant bank of the river receded into darkness as their residents climbed into bed. The city was never entirely quiet; at night it hummed softly beyond the trees in the distance, but the many pieces of this urban puzzle melted and oozed into each other. Its various sounds became indistinguishable.

David felt entirely alone and discarded. The heavy, humid air threatened to suffocate him, as though some invisible hand from above were holding a pillow over his face. Memories of home, however frustrating or imperfect, seemed safe and welcoming against the backdrop of this vast, uncaring urban misery. Far from being a maze of endless opportunity for this small-town boy, it seemed for the first time like a boundless cesspool where you had to fight to stay afloat.

Humid daylight arose over the city, but David couldn't remember seeing it creep up from behind the trees. He wasn't sure how or when he got there, but he caught himself walking in a despondent haze past the red neon lettering of a bank in Chinatown. David looked like a slight, wretched figure against the grand, shining sign — slighter still as he slunk beneath the ornate Royal Arch. The smell of recycled cooking oil mixed with the fragrant steam from bubbling cauldrons of broth travelled through the air. The doors of shops and family-run grocery stores opened. Neon tube lights flickered. Civil servants with identification cards hanging from necks and pinned to belts hurried to their offices while weather-beaten shopkeepers, abiding by a daily routine — an unchanged routine that spanned decades — pushed carts of fresh vegetables down Somerset. On a patio, young men in skinny jeans and black-rimmed glasses, with just the right amount of facial hair, goji berry smoothies and an abundance of time commiserated smartly about the nature of privilege.

***

"Jesus, you look like shit." Franco's words displayed a mix of irritation and genuine concern.

"Yeah, I had that cheeseburger you suggested. The eleven bucks was even enough for me to supersize it." Bitter resentment tinged David's every word.

"I'm sensing a tone and I don't appreciate it, David…" Franco stared at the scrawny kid — clearly hungover — through his tinted glasses.

David slammed Franco's desk with his right hand.

"Hey, what do you say to this Frankie: If I suck off some old pervert, can you give me a twenty?" He glared at Franco, who sat back in his chair and observed the boy for a few seconds before speaking.

"Okay, fine. I get it: you're pissed. There's a washroom down the hall. Go wipe yourself up. You're useless to me like this. Today's a new day, Shakespeare, but you need to work with me dammit! Don't lose faith!"

***

David emerged from the sink and stared at himself in the mirror. The refrain from "Snow White" — "Mirror, mirror, on the wall" — bounced about inside his head annoyingly. He looked tired, with dark circles around eyes that bore an almost lifeless expression. In the background, yellowed wallpaper adorned with red and green grapes covered the thin wall. Grapes made David think immediately of Dame Wanda, spread across the sofa. He could hear Franco carrying on a heated telephone conversation on the other side of that thin wall.

"I told you not to open the door! You don't have to accept that letter from him … no, I know that it won't make it go away. But work with me, Lina! For God's sake, work with me … yeah, I know, I know." Franco paused, before his voice rose in exasperation. "Who said anything about having to pay legal fees? Did I ever say that? Well, did I? Fuck no, I didn't, and you know it!"

David closed the tap and listened intently.

"Well we don't have any kids, so why are you bringing that up? Why are you worrying about that now? Look, I said I'll sort it out. You don't need to freak out about it. I'm expecting a deposit to hit the account any minute. We'll be fine … yeah, I promise." Franco's voice softened. "I promise…"

David wiped his hands on his pants and returned to the office.

"Everything okay?" David felt as though he had a duty to strike a compassionate, caring tone with Franco, who seemed preoccupied with his phone. Franco looked decidedly stressed but forced a smile.

"No need to worry about me, Shakespeare. You've got enough on your shoulders as it is. Besides, things are looking up! And I mean really up! I have a friend who owns a sandwich factory. He supplies all the government cafeterias and convenience stores in town." Franco seemed satisfied with himself.

"I have to make sandwiches?"

"That's right, Shakespeare!" Franco got up from his chair and sat on the edge of the desk facing an incredulous David.

"Egg salad, tuna salad, salmon salad, hummus and veggies for the granolas; the whole gamut. But don't worry, it's only temporary. Just while I find something better; it will put a few more dollars in your pocket than you've seen in the last little while. You know, just to tide you over."

***

It was more of a sterile laboratory than a kitchen: some type of subterranean workshop with low ceilings, blinding neon lighting, metal tables and work surfaces that seemed more becoming to an autopsy room. There was not a person in sight. David mechanically plopped scoops of tuna fish onto white bread, one after the other, as the refrigerator hummed. He had been given a white lab coat to wear, along with a hairnet and surgical gloves. Every quarter of an hour, the PA system blared, breaking the monotony. A lifeless male voice spoke in an oddly transatlantic accent.

"Your safety is our number-one priority. In case of an accident or emergency in your kitchen, please press the red panic button located on the side. Do not enter another employee's kitchen area. Do not disturb your colleagues while they are at work. Your cellphones do not have reception in our kitchens. Please rely on the panic button. Do not panic, assistance is on its way."

The PA system fell silent and David began mindlessly chopping cucumbers. Instructions appearing on a flat-screen television above his work area informed him of the sandwiches he was to produce next. It was granola time. As he completed each batch, he packed Cellophane-wrapped sandwiches in boxes, placed these into the dumbwaiter and pressed the big green button next to the door. The sandwiches made their way up to freedom from this clinical underground lair.

David's thoughts started to drift off to nowhere, his exhausted eyes glazed over, before being rudely awakened by the transatlantic man in the speaker.

"Attention, attention! We are now seventy-five percent through the workday and have reached fifty percent of our daily sandwich production target. Please speed up. Please speed up. *Please, speed up!* We thank you for your enthusiasm."

"Okay, that's it!" David peeled off the surgical gloves, tore off his hairnet and climbed out of his lab coat. He hurried from the kitchen to a bland office, where a landline phone sat untouched and soundless on the metal desk.

By now, he knew Franco's number by heart. Admittedly, it wasn't hard to memorize: 613–777–LUCK.

"Franco? Good, you picked up..." David breathed a sigh of relief. "Am I getting paid today? It's the fourth day. I really need the money now ... But you promised me eleven dollars an hour! I've been here eight hours a day ... No, I never see the boss. I don't *know* why he never shows up. I barely see anyone else working here. We're all in these separate little kitchens. Almost like little cubicles or laboratories. It's pretty weird, Franco. I don't know what to make of it. I really need that money tonight. *Please!* I need to pay my cellphone bill and finally call home. Okay, okay ... Great. Can you meet me this evening? Do you want me to come to you? No? ... Well, I'll send you the directions in a text."

***

At his campsite, David could barely hear the music of Tim Buckley emanating from the public beach beneath the voices of a half-dozen men and women sitting in a circle passing around a joint and a bottle of rum. He put on his best polo shirt and waited anxiously, wondering if Franco would actually arrive with his pay. He was ten minutes late and David's stomach was becoming a knotted mess. If he didn't get paid today, he'd have no choice but to stand in line tomorrow at the soup kitchen, and that would seal his fate. It would turn his adventurous, youthful camping trip on the edge of town and his stab at building a new life into a state of homelessness. And David knew that homelessness was neither youthful nor adventurous, but simply hopeless, tired and undignified.

The branches and leaves rustled, and since there was no breeze on that stuffy, sticky evening, David realized that it must be Franco making his way to the camp. Sure enough, Franco, in his signature blazer, with cellphone in hand and eyes peeking out from the top of those tinted glasses, emerged from the woods and looked genuinely perplexed.

"Jesus. This is where you live?" Franco looked around briefly before returning swiftly to the purpose of his visit. Whatever was happening in David's life was unfortunate, but he didn't want to get deeply involved. "Here you go, Shakespeare. You've been doing good. Real good." Franco handed David an envelope and turned around as quickly as he could to leave.

"Forty dollars?" David held up two twenties and looked at Franco in exasperation. "Where's the rest?"

"There was a little glitch at the bank, Dave. No need to worry about it though. I'll have it sorted by tomorrow, Davey."

"A glitch?" David found his bearings and laughed scornfully. "Sounds to me like *you're* a glitch!"

"What did you just say?" Franco walked up close to David and removed his glasses.

"Oh, sorry. Let me put it in clearer language: you're a fuck-up!" David was beginning to relish this exchange — maybe even more than if he had just been paid what he was owed.

"Excuse me?" All show and pretense were gone. Franco sounded genuinely taken aback.

"You're a *stain* on the fabric of society. You're like the guy in a polyester suit sitting behind the desk in the lobby of a cheap hotel, renting out rooms by the hour to burnt-out hookers, with nothing but big dreams to keep him alive!"

Franco looked both astounded and enraged. He pushed David but didn't manage to get him to fall to the ground. In the midst of an adrenaline rush that made him feel simply fantastic, David grabbed Franco, put him into a headlock and tightened until Franco's face turned the colour of a beet. Franco struggled, tried to use his hands to claw himself out of the lock, heaved and huffed and groaned like a cornered wild animal, before giving in.

"Okay, okay! *Please!*" David felt satiated and let him go. Franco stumbled away to a corner of the campsite, hunched over as he spat, tried to catch his breath and regain his composure. He wiped the sweat from his face with his sleeve before turning to David, who was rummaging in his backpack. David retrieved a bottle of sparking wine and had the glow of a man who had just struck gold. He unwrapped the purple aluminum on the neck of the bottle and pulled the cork with skill and ease.

Franco looked confused and beat.

"What exactly are we celebrating?"

"Here, it will make you feel better..." David passed Franco the bottle and motioned for him to sit next to him on a log. Franco reluctantly took a gulp, sat down and passed the bottle back to David without making eye contact.

"I guess it's my turn to ask questions..."

Franco offered no response and continued staring at the water in front of them. He was visibly deflated.

"How long were you going to have me work at that sandwich place before paying me, or telling me that there's no money?"

Franco bore the expression of a petulant child who had been caught. He sulked quietly and continued staring at the water.

"How many people have you duped so far, Franco?"

He turned to David and his expression transformed into one of resentfulness.

"I don't dupe people, David."

David laughed dismissively.

"Okay. I see. So how long have you been keeping up this charade, Franco? It's not so much that I'm angry with you anymore, but I *am* curious."

"That just shows how little you understand. Charade, lifestyle, image, perception. Can you tell me the difference between them?" Franco took the bottle of sparking wine from David and chugged it.

"I've been through some tough times even back home. *I know.*"

"You know squat, Shakespeare. Everything happens on a different scale in the city. And on this scale, you can't see the end of the road, whether you're going up or whether you're going down — it's endless either way." Franco set his eyes on the river again. As the sun descended, the waters looked as though they were pure, flowing gold.

David's mood, first anger and irritation, then aggression, changed again. The adrenaline rush mostly subsided.

"You should write that down. It's pretty good." David smiled faintly and tapped against the bottle.

"Like Margaret Laurence's diviners, all of us on the periphery of respectable society are collecting, sorting and hunting through garbage, looking for clues and treasures about this mysterious, multi-faceted, brutal, uncaring, unlivable, yet somehow mesmerizing society ... *in the garbage.* It helps us understand. And if you understand, you can probably learn how to cope..."

He thought that his literary life-coaching monologue was superior to anything Franco had offered him over the past week. But David had become so lost in the imagery of it all, in the underappreciated work of divining, that he didn't notice Franco remove his blazer, shoes, watch and wallet with surgical dispassion and precision, and walk away a few feet in the direction of the river.

By the time David finally looked up, Franco had removed his shirt and pants and was facing the river, with a determined pose and expression.

"Franco? What the hell are you doing?"

Franco looked back at David with a fierce stare. He seemed hell-bent, angry and hurt.

"What's going on? Are you okay?" David was confused and concerned — but not enough to walk up to Franco and stop him as he walked slowly into the river.

"You know, if you don't answer me, I could just walk away with all your stuff. Money, cards, clothing. *Everything.*" David had hoped that this would be sufficient to get Franco's attention. But picking up his wallet, he saw that it was empty, except for a five-dollar bill, a credit card that had expired two years prior, the business card of a psychic and a receipt from a Chinese restaurant. By the time David looked up, Franco had walked five metres from the bank into the river.

"Franco? Franco!"

The water rippled and bubbled as Franco dunk his head in.

He had walked so far out into the river that the water eventually came up to his neck. He seemed little more than a fading, nameless blob in the distance. David couldn't tell if Franco was swimming or just floating, passively allowing the water to carry him further out, whichever way. A sound that resembled the heavily amplified ding of a microwave startled

David. He noticed that Franco's cellphone had lit up with a message from his wife, Lina.

"Franco, what the hell? Where are you? The bank has been calling non-stop. We need to talk, *now!*"

The phone felt sticky, and David noticed that the screen was badly cracked. He paced back and forth from his tent to the water for a full minute before responding. He felt troubled and excited all at once. But after brief deliberation, he realized that finally, his time had come.

"My dearest Lina, I have decided to go for an evening dip. I am presently swimming with the current — he has proven to be a surprisingly sweet friend and of fine temper. I anticipate an on-time arrival to my destination, just prior to sundown. Do go ahead and dine without me tonight. I shall either feast on a canopy of soft seaweed on the ocean floor or, God willing, on a nocturnal banquet fit for a king. I am told that the siren Gabriella, the high cherub of the sea, shall keep me company tonight. My good chap the current, though allegedly a heathen, promises to assist with the repartee. Oh heavens, I am afraid I must be off now, my darling! The current is becoming testy. Please give my love to the cat. F.R."

David felt so much better. Had he found his calling? But the dream world he had concocted — in high diction, no less — came crashing down to reality when Bob the radio announcer, in his congenial valley accent, took to the air.

"Oh, what a ride it's been folks! Not for the faint of heart; but as you know, we're all about the straight talk. No sugar-coating, just good old-fashioned honesty. We need more of that in this world of ours. Now then ... it's going to be a steamy night. Crack open that window or turn on the AC. Good night, tomorrow's comin'."

About the Author

Christopher Adam was born in Montreal but spent his formative years during the nineties in Budapest, Hungary. Upon returning to Canada, he completed his undergraduate studies in history and English literature at Concordia University, before continuing with graduate studies at Carleton and completing a PhD in history at the University of Ottawa. He launched and continues to edit two award-winning online publications offering analysis and commentary on current affairs in Europe.

Over the last fifteen years, Ottawa has become home. By day Christopher works in the non-governmental organization sector. By night he teaches and writes — and somewhere in between, he travels as much as possible.